I'm 13 Years Old
And I Changed The World

D.K. Brantley

Obviously, because this is a work of fiction, the names, places, and events in this book are either the product of the author's imagination or are used fictitiously. Any type of resemblance to real life is relatively coincidental, so please don't sue.

Published by Sir Brody Books
Cleveland, Tennessee USA
sirbrody.com

Printed in the United States of America

Cover Art by Vlad C. Diegys

Edited by Jessica Brantley

For Dylan

one

I ride home with Mom after school, still a bit shocked. Dad has a job, Mom and Dad kissed in front of my entire class, Noelle was touched by my parents' smooch, and the school year is over. It's a lot to take in, and I ride in silence trying to figure out which part is most worthy of my attention.

But it's no use. I think of all of them at once, my brain hopping from the kiss to Dad's new job to Noelle's look of "Aaaahhh!" and back again. As we approach Grandpa's driveway, an ambulance pulls up to Big Mike's. Its lights are on, but the sirens are silent.

The back doors pop open and an EMT hops out and helps another inside the ambulance lower a stretcher to the ground.

Mrs. Jackson climbs out and holds the arm of a thin creature who looks vaguely familiar.

I wave.

A weak voice calls out from the stretcher.

"Adam! Hey, man—school out?"

"Yeah, school's out," I say, unsure whose voice it is.

I move toward the stretcher.

Mrs. Jackson smiles.

I look down.

Wearing a powder blue hospital gown is a creature that was once the terror of PMS.

"Mike?"

two

"Mike?" I repeat in a cracked whisper.

He wheezes. "Didn't expect to see me or something?"

I attempt a laugh. What I didn't expect was to see him looking like a stretcher full of bones with skin hanging wherever it fell. After months of buying into the hype that Big Mike was at military academy in some distant desert, getting yelled at for not spit-shining his shoes just right, I imagined him coming back a little thicker and even a bit meaner, ready to remind everyone at Palmetto Middle that the name Big Mike isn't just a reflection of his physical size. It matches his one-two punching combo as well.

Mike smiles, coughs, and winces.

"You okay?" I ask.

Mike's head doesn't sport the high-and-tight crew cut of the military academy. Instead, it mimics that of an elderly man whose hair grows where it wants and abandons hope elsewhere.

"I'll be all right," he says.

"Sorry to interrupt, boys," Mrs. Jackson says, "but Michael needs to get inside. It's safer for him there."

Safer?

Big Mike shrugs awkwardly.

"See you tomorrow," Mike says.

I hesitate.

"Yeah, Mike," I say with a nod. "See you tomorrow."

"Good. I wanna hear how the school year ended—whether you finally got Noelle's attention."

three

My face burns as I walk away.

Images of Big Mike in a powder blue hospital gown (kind of weird thinking of Mike in any kind of gown) disappear and all I see is my lady. Okay, she's not quite my lady. But you know—the lady who will one day be my lady. Anyway, all I can see is her smile cutting through space and time just for me. I reach out to hold her hand, and—

HONK!

A mad woman stares me down, her left arm waving through the open window of her minivan. I stare back, trying to figure out if I've seen her before.

She sticks her head out the window to give me

a better view.

"Can you get out of the way, please?" she asks sarcastically.

I'm in the middle of the street. Not sure how long I've been here, but when a guy gets in that Noelle trance, it could be hours, days, years.

I mumble an apology, tuck my hair behind my ears, and speed home. I climb the steps to Grandpa's front door as the van's brakes cry with the effort of stopping. I turn and watch Mike's weird little cousin Z pop out of the van and zip to Big Mike's. The front door opens before Z knocks even once. Mrs. Jackson welcomes him in and waves the crazed van driver goodbye.

Mom, Dad, and Grandpa are in the living room. They stop talking when I come in, view me with Big Mike-sized sadness. Sadness I've not seen or felt since Dad lost his job, we moved to Grandpa's place, and Mom and Dad's marriage hit the endangered species list before making a dramatic comeback, thanks to me.

"You okay?" Mom asks.

I look at her, measure the question.

"Sure," I say. "Shouldn't I be?"

Mom's hands tighten around her knees and she

rocks nervously. Dad shifts uncomfortably. Grandpa takes a deep breath, holds it, holds it, holds it…exhales.

"She's just worried about you, Adam," Grandpa says. "We all are. Worried about you, worried about Michael. It's hard to see somebody dealing with cancer."

I step back.

"Cancer?"

All of Mom's worry focuses on me.

"Do you know what cancer is?" she asks.

Yes, Mom, I know what cancer is. Cells grow out of control and ruin people's lives. There's treatment, it usually doesn't work, and whoever winds up with the cancer winds up dead.

But cancer only hits old people and strangers. It doesn't affect kids. Not normal kids. And especially not huge piles of muscle like Big Mike. Those guys get in fights, go to military school, and come back with new skills. They don't get cancer.

But I don't say any of this. My legs are too weak, my voice unreliable.

"How do you know?" I ask, scanning their faces to make sure this isn't some sick joke. It can't be though. I saw Big Mike, and he's definitely sick. Very sick. Cancer sick.

Mom looks at Dad, who looks at Grandpa, who looks at me.

"We found out a few weeks ago," Grandpa says. "Your father found out from his boss."

"Your boss told you?" I ask, my voice leaping from my throat.

"Yes," Dad admits. "Mr. Hart found out that Michael is battling leukemia. Met him at the hospital. I didn't know when or how to tell you. I kept waiting for the right time."

four

"Adam, wake up, sweetheart. Adam Shannon!"

I wake up to Mom tapping, pecking, pushing my shoulder. The sun breaks through the living room window, covers the couch, and comes to a rest just before the door of the bedroom I share with my grandfather. I sit up on the rug that has been in the middle of Grandpa's living room since the dawn of time.

"Was I sleeping?"

"You passed out, Shannon," Dad says.

That explains the throbbing headache and Mom's expression.

I get to my feet and amble into the bathroom. In the mirror, I watch the bump on my forehead work its way from a molehill into a mountain. The surrounding skin is already abandoning its normal pinkish tint, and I picture the future of my forehead: greens, purples, reds, and blues coming together as one big, happy family. I shut the door, toss the toilet lid down, and have a seat.

The last time I cried was one of the rare times Mom and Dad let me watch a movie. I was nine years old, and the movie involved a boxer named Rocky Balboa and his son, Robert. Well, now there's a new last-time-I-cried moment.

My bathroom time comes to an abrupt end when the oldest guy in the house bangs on the door and says he has to use it. There's only one bathroom in this place, and I've been using it to whimper and snot all over myself.

I clear my throat. Twice.

"Almost done!"

I run the sink and splash water on my face. As I towel it dry, I scan the mirror. Looks like I've been crying in the rain. Perfect.

Fortunately, Mom and Dad let me beeline it to bed. They don't call my name, ask any questions, make any noise to indicate they want to talk. I get under the covers in my clothes and bury my head under the pillow.

Over Grandpa's bathroom grunts, a familiar sound cuts through the layers of blankets and pillows. Muffled by the bedroom walls, Mom's jerky cries leap into my ear, joined by a deeper cry that sporadically escapes Dad's chest.

With my face pressed into the pillow, I take stock of my situation.

I just spent the better part of a school year trying to save my parents from getting divorced, and now I've got to beat cancer? Scientists have been trying to do it for years, so I doubt I can do it before it's too late for Mike. But I have to. Or I have to do something. What that something is, I'm not sure, and crying makes a man tired.

five

I transfer a pile of eggs from one side of my plate to the other and back again as I explain that Big Mike really does want me to come over. Mom and Dad suspect he may not be up for the challenge of entertaining me. That maybe he was just being polite.

I shovel in a mouthful of sausage, put down my fork, cross my arms, and stare at them across the table. They, in turn, sigh with the timing of a synchronized swimming team.

Dad shrugs.

"Fine with me," he says. "Just don't stick around if he looks tired."

*****

A dozen knocks later, the door opens at Big Mike's house.

"Oh, hey, Z—Mike wanted to hang out today."

Z's typical frightened expression has turned sad. He hands me something and ducks behind the door. It's a blue surgical mask.

I shrug and put it on.

Mike's house is as dark as usual, the lights looming uselessly overhead. As I enter his room, a strange lady exits. She's got short blonde hair with red streaks for good measure. She pulls off her own surgical mask and smiles one of those grown-up smiles built for comfort.

"I'll see you at your next treatment, Mike," she promises over her shoulder.

Mrs. Jackson, who is in a chair beside Big Mike's bed, speaks through her mask.

"What do you say, son?"

"Thank you." Mike's voice is distorted by his mask, but the sarcasm cuts straight through it.

"I'll make a gentleman out of you yet!" Mike's mother stands up and presses her face against his forehead, a surgical mask the only barrier between her lips and her son's skin. "You boys be good."

"We will, Mom."

Big Mike watches his mom leave the room and rolls his eyes so far back in his head I fear he's dead. Before I yell for help, he whispers excitedly in that kindergartner whisper he's mastered.

"You see that blonde? Ai, ai, ai!"

"You're drooling, Mike," I say. "I can see it pooling in your mask. And besides, she's at least 900 years older than you."

Okay, that's an exaggeration, but adults don't fall in love with middle school students. Not without jail time.

"Age knows no love!" Mike says confidently. He screws up his eyes, pinches them shut, and self-corrects: "Love knows no age—age. Yeah, that's it. Anyway, what's up with your head?"

"My head?" I swipe my hand across my forehead and feel tenderness all over. "Oh yeah. Got a bump on there, I guess. Nothing major."

Big Mike shrugs. I give him a high-flying fist bump and crash into the chair his mom left vacant.

"So what's up with your dramatic entrance yesterday?"

"You mean the ambulance?" Mike says. "Pretty slick, wasn't it? Mom didn't want to leave me even for a second, so when I got transferred to the big hospital in Franklin for surgery, she rode in the ambulance with me. When it was time to come home, her car was still at Palmetto Memorial, so they piled us into the back of the ambulance again. Not a real big deal, but I bet it was impressive to see. Would've been cooler if they had the sirens running, but they wouldn't do it. Turned on the lights for me though. Had to let everybody know I was back."

six

We hang out for half an hour before Mike's eyes slide shut and he falls asleep in front of me. Doesn't even try to fight it off.

I slip out of his room, wave good-bye to his mom, and head across the street. It's ten in the morning and the sun shines fiercely—a stark contrast to the dark world from which I emerge, a world in which a strong, happy, healthy middle school kid turns into a punching bag for a disease that should be reserved for old folks.

"Hey, Shannon, how'd it go over there?"

"Fine," I say, opting for the classic, one-size-fits-all response.

Dad views me with a cocked eyebrow.

"Fine?"

"He got tired pretty fast, so I came home. Guess it's expected with the leukemia and chemo."

An itch reminds me I'm wearing a mask, and I yank it off. A sudden urge to cry strikes—Am I becoming a pansy?—so I go to my bedroom, thankful Grandpa is at the Senior Center doing old people aerobics. The rest of my world is confusing and changing, but at least this twin mattress is still the same.

When I wake up, Grandpa stares at me.

Welcome to Creepyville.

"Adam—good news!"

I sit up, expecting to hear that Noelle, the gorgeous curly-headed beauty at Palmetto Middle School, wants to go steady with me. Or maybe my parents have decided it's time to swap out that ridiculous you-can-only-call-your-parents cell phone for something with a touch screen. Or does it have to do with Big Mike?

"Follow me," he says quietly.

I leap out of bed, look for my shoes only to realize they're still on my feet, and follow my loafer-wearing granddad. He leads out the front door and waves his arms like Vanna White showing the next puzzle on Wheel of Fortune.

I scan the area for something worth seeing. All I see is the same old neighborhood looking like it's always looked. My shoulders slump when Grandpa's hands grip either side of my head. He forces my head down and to the left, to that old-fashioned lawn mower that made me sweat more last fall than I've sweat in my life.

"That's it?"

Fantastic. Grandpa's big surprise is a relic that he decided to use as decoration for the front yard.

"That's it!" he says with more cheer than necessary. "Seems the leaves wore the blades out on this beauty, so I got them sharpened. Should make your job a little easier."

I squint at the mower and then at Grandpa, who flashes a twenty-dollar bill at me. I don't need the money like I did before, but a fella can always find a way to spend a few bucks.

After nearly an eternity, I finish cutting the grass and head inside. Every pore of my being is doused in salty wetness. It drips into my mouth, stings my eyes, makes my socks squishy.

"Looks good, Adam."

Mom leans against the kitchen counter, holding out a glass of clear sports drink. I take it, swallowing the whole thing in a continuous slurp.

seven

Big Mike laughs. It's a weak laugh, but he puts everything he has into it.

"Your granddad's cheap friend bought it. That doesn't count—it shouldn't have sold at all!"

"Hey," I say, "the deal was that I get to call you Tiny if the Garfield glass sold for less than $12, and it did. I don't care what you think about it, Tiny!"

Big Mike—Tiny for the day—coughs and points at me for emphasis.

"Least I wasn't out sweating buckets with that old lawn mower."

"You watched me?"

Tiny pulls a string attached to his blinds. They

fly open to a perfect view of my grandfather's front yard. Seems the one-time Sasquatch has been watching me from across the street.

"Like my technique?" I ask, pushing an imaginary reel mower back and forth across the hardwood floors in Mike's room.

"You're forgetting something," Tiny says. He wipes his forehead and tosses a world of imaginary sweat to the ground, his head bobbing from one side to the other uncontrollably.

I release my imaginary mower and double over. Eventually, I gain enough composure to ask the obvious: "You were creeping on me mowing the lawn? What took you so long to say something?"

Big Mike stifles himself and puts on the straightest face he can. "Timing." With that, he laughs again. I join in, wondering if he's laughing at me or with me.

A moment later, Mike sighs and asks about my crush on Noelle. I ask about his crush on—well…if he has an age-appropriate crush. According to Big Mike, he doesn't need to go after girls. He gets to sort through them and pick the best.

"Sure, Mike," I say. "I'm sure they'd go gaga over you now."

Mike inspects his thinned arms, runs his hands

through his wispy hair, lets his feet shift left and then right under the covers. His face droops and he looks me square in the eye.

"I'm still Mike, Adam. Not even cancer can take that away." He pauses long enough to make me feel like a jerk. "And the ladies still love me."

I pull the pillow out from under his head and smash him on the face one, two, three good hits. We both hold our stomachs from laughter, and I wipe moisture from the creases of my eyes.

I stick around until he starts to get that I-know-you're-here-but-I'm-so-tired-I-don't-really-care look. Instead of waiting for him to fall asleep, I give him a fist bump and head out.

"We need a system," Tiny says, his eyes sleepy slivers.

"A system?"

"Some way for you to know when it's okay to come over. You know," he says, "so you don't interrupt me and the nurse..."

"When she's cleaning your puke bucket?"

"Yeah. Or something like that. And so you'll know when I'm awake and you're clear to come over." He thinks, wrinkling his every facial feature in the process. Then he yells with the force of someone about to pass out: "Z! Clean underwear!"

As if on standby for Mike's every need, a masked Z weaves between the door frame and me with boxers in hand. The Oakland Athletics logo is emblazoned all over them, and the waistband is large enough to fit around a mature oak tree.

Fast as he appears, Z vanishes.

"You like the A's? They stink!" I say. "Pun intended."

"I don't like the A's," Mike—Tiny for the day—says. "But when they had Canseco, McGuire, the Hendersons—Dave and Rickey—Eckersley, Stewart…"

"Okay, okay! I get it!"

Tiny lazily leans over and shoves the man-sized boxers against the window. The blinds crinkle and threaten to break. I cringe at the scraping sound.

"You see these, all is clear." Mike is flat on his back again, his eyes fully closed. "Got it?"

"Got it." I consider giving the once-big guy a hug, think better of it, and leave.

eight

A large pair of boxer shorts that read "Athletics" in green and gold stare at me from across the street. I choke down a quick breakfast, toss on a pair of shorts and a t-shirt, and head out to see Mike.

His mom answers the door with a worried look. My "Good morning, Mrs. Jackson" is met with silence. As I step into Big Mike's room, the front door creaks to a slow close.

Mike is propped up against his headboard. He looks an inch closer to health than the day before, but he wears a version of his mom's concern.

"Hey, Mike—what's up?"

He snaps out of the staring contest he's having

with the wall.

"You okay?" I ask.

Mike tilts his English Mastiff head to the side. I hear the gears turn slowly, painfully in his head.

"Yeah. You?"

I take a seat on the chair next to Mike's bed. He leans toward an empty bucket in his lap and freezes in the puke position.

"It's Z." Big Mike's eyes focus on the bottom of the bucket. "Z's mom. She's having some problems."

nine

There are worse ways to spend a hot summer day. I'm in front of a TV with Josh, John, and Sam—my lunch crew from Palmetto Middle School (a.k.a. PMS)—playing video games. Or they play. I sit and watch and sidestep their occasional question about Big Mike. I don't see any need to poop on their party. Besides, it's nice to not think about cancer for a few hours.

While they shoot zombies, race make-believe creatures in high-tech race cars, and work together to save the planet from certain destruction via video game controllers, they laugh about the good life. For them, the good life is summer vacation without the hassle of summer reading.

There was a time, a very terrible time, when un-suspecting children were forced to read books every summer. When school came screaming toward them at the end of summer break, all those helpless students had to give an accounting of what they read (or didn't read).

No more!

Thanks to students who came before us and re-fused to finish their summer reading, our board of ed-ucation threw up their hands in frustration and brought summer reading to a screeching halt. After all, if stu-dents aren't going to read and teachers aren't allowed to give them bad grades, what's the point?

From my perspective, this is great news. It means I get to read what I want. And it probably won't be some book written for middle schoolers. From the lunch crew's perspective, it's great news for another reason altogether: more time to waste in front of a screen.

But enough about that. I'm starting to sound like my parents.

After this fascinating day, John's mom drops me off at home. I tramp through the living room and see Mom hovering over a small, elementary school-sized creature. She's not quite chewing up food and spitting it into his mouth like a mother bird, but she may as well be.

"Oh, hi, Adam!"

Mom sets a glass of milk down and reaches toward me for a hug. The stranger turns, and I look Z in the eyes. I couldn't be more confused if I suddenly had Big Mike's deep voice.

"Thought we'd have Simon over," Mom says. "Good to know the neighbors, don't you think?"

Did mom just call Z Simon?

"Yeah," I say, more a question than an answer. I turn and make my way to the bedroom I share with Grandpa. On the way, I scan the scene across the street. No boxer shorts.

I spend twenty minutes attempting to read Ulysses, but it doesn't make sense. And the background noise in my head isn't helping.

Z is sitting in my kitchen.

With my Mom.

I don't know if Mom invited him over or picked him up off the side of the street, but Z's startled expression says he's as uncomfortable as usual. So at least that was normal. But why did Mom call him Simon?

AND I CHANGED THE WORLD

A knock breaks my trance.

"Yeah?"

Mom pushes open the door.

I sigh, mumble for her to come in.

She sandwiches my hands between her own. My eyebrows go higher and higher until they hover just below the Himalayas. Mom tightens her grip, nearly squeezing every ounce of life force from my hands.

Her eyes strain. Tears bubble to the surface.

Finally, when she can't press any tighter, she gives one final squeeze, kisses me on the cheek, says she loves me.

She walks out, leaving one of her tears on my cheek. It tickles, but I resist the urge to wipe it away.

ten

As I shuffle across the street, Big Mike raises his blinds and signals for me to come in. I skip the knock at Mike's request and tiptoe to his room.

"Close the door."

I reach back for the door, when Mrs. Jackson and Z jump out and yell.

"Surprise!"

I fall to the floor. Mrs. Jackson and Z look startled behind their surgical masks.

"Couldn't have said it better myself," I say. "Surprise for what?" I get to my feet, push my mask back into place.

I look at Mike's mom. Nothing. The same from

Z. The only person with any kind of expression is Mike, and it's buried under a mask.

"I may be stuck in bed," Mike says, "but I know when my buddy's birthday arrives."

"My mom told you, didn't she?"

"No way!" Mike crosses his arms for a moment, then points at Z. "Your mom told him."

Honestly, I don't care how Mike found out. When you're scrawny, have hair your parents won't let you cut, and a name like Adam Shannon Dakota Carr, just having someone care that it's your birthday is nice. Make the guy who cares a one-time brute who made even teachers shudder, and yeah—it's pretty great.

Even greater when the brute hands over a present. Unlike the argyle socks I got from Mom and Dad, I'm sure this will be something I want.

"Mom thought you'd like it," Mike says with a cough.

"I'm sure I will."

Mrs. Jackson looks on, her eyes slanting with happiness. Z stares his Z stare. Or is it a Simon stare?

I finger the tape on the edges of the gift and wrack my brain for something to say. Having Mike's mom and Z stand at attention throws me off of my gift game.

"Open the present!" Big Mike yells.

I tug at the wrapping paper when the gift is snatched from my hands.

"It's not glass! Open it like this!" Mike grabs the loose paper and charades a massive, powerful pull before handing the package back to me.

I get the box open on my lap faster than you can say, "I hope that present really isn't glass." And it isn't.

It's a shirt. Perfect. Just what every middle school dudes wants: clothes. I let my eyes bulge in what I hope is convincing excitement and whip out the shirt for inspection.

It's black with a white silhouette of a guy jumping, arms and legs spread eagle, the phrase, "I Wanna Be Like Mike" emblazoned in red.

"Who wouldn't want to be like me?" Mike presses his once-gigantic barrel chest out and eyes his biceps. As a final testament to his perceived good looks, he runs his hands across his partially bald scalp. "Wish you had this head of hair, don't you?"

I push him, tipping him over backward. Mrs. Jackson releases months of tension with a single laugh. Z shakes with a frightened expression.

"You were tough stuff a few months ago, but there's a new sheriff in town." I lift my shirtsleeves to show my arms. Somehow, they shrink when I flex. "Hmmm…looks like the boys could use some work."

I hit the floor for a dozen quick push-ups. More than I've done since being forced into that government-mandated Presidential Physical Fitness Test. I stand up and hop from one foot to the next.

"Nice form," Mike says. "Mom really enjoyed it."

"Oh, Michael," Mrs. Jackson says. "Don't embarrass Adam. It's good to see him doing what he can to get healthy. Now you need to do the same."

Mike gives a questioning glance to his mom, who reminds him that his next treatment is in the morning, and he'll need his energy for recovery.

"Hang tomorrow?" he asks.

Mrs. Jackson raises an eyebrow.

"Well," Mike says, "soon?"

I promise to keep an eye out for the A's.

eleven

There's been no sign of Mike for a couple days. I mow the lawn, wondering if he's watching me sweat my way across the brittle July grass. I finish the job and put up the mower, considering what to do with the cash Grandpa is bound to give me for another stellar job.

As I close the garage door, Mom calls.

"Coming!"

I sit soaking, sopping wet at the kitchen table, a pale purple sports drink in hand.

"I got a call from Michael's mother," Mom says. "Michael would like you to come over soon. Today if you're up for it."

Up for it? How hard can it be to walk across the street and hang out in an air-conditioned house?

"Yeah," I say. "I can do that. Would have gone earlier, but—well...we ummm...have a system, and..."

"A system?" Mom turns her head curiously, attempting to bait an answer out of me. No can do. "Anyway," she says, "Mrs. Jackson says he's not doing real well at the moment. Apparently he's getting hit pretty hard by chemotherapy."

Chemotherapy. I've read all about the stuff. It's intentional poisoning. A doctor inserts a port in the patient's body and funnels highly toxic medication through it into the patient's body. This medication's mission: attack cancerous cells and leave the others alone.

Unfortunately, it usually attacks everything in its path, and the patient suffers some pretty nasty side effects as a result. Mike's new hairdo is one of them. As is weakness, fatigue, puking all the time—essentially what you hear about on radio commercials for diarrhea medication. Speaking of the cha-chas, that's one of the side effects. Yep. Chemo'll give you the squirts, too.

Anyway, I've read about it. So I'm prepared for

whatever comes my way. Or rather…Mike's way.

I take a final swig from my drink, wipe my mouth, and slam the glass down. "Sounds good," I say.

Mom clears her throat.

"Forgetting something?"

I run through a mental list of things I need to take to Mike's and only come up with one thing: me.

"Don't think so, Mom."

"A shower, maybe?"

twelve

Mrs. Jackson walks out of Mike's room with a finger to her mask. I look past her, where Mike is sleeping. I quietly tell her I'll come back later.

"Oh no," she says. "He'd love if you were here when he wakes up."

She pats my arm and pulls me back into Mike's room. The straight-back chair by his bed has been replaced with a big blue recliner.

Mrs. Jackson points to a cardboard box by the chair.

"Enjoy," she whispers.

The box teems with color and art—art I've been told to avoid. Art my parents claim isn't on the level of Michelangelo, storytelling that isn't on par with Faulkner. Of course, Dad has a small stash of comics from his youth, but that's different, right?

I lift the first in the pile. Tape that once held the plastic sleeve closed hangs limply from overuse. The book slides easily into my left hand.

"Didn't know you liked comic books."

Mike adjusts his mask, rubs his eyes.

"You didn't know I liked comic books?" I ask. "I didn't know you could read!"

"They're my dad's. Well—the older ones are," he says. "And I can't read. That's why I like comics."

A sick feeling grows in the pit of my stomach. Big Mike can't read?

"You're so easy, Shannon!"

"What did you call me?"

"Shannon," Mike repeats. "And you deserve it! You think I can't read? What kind of moron you think I am?"

I throw a punch at him. Were it not for my superhuman muscle control, the impact would knock him into next year. As it is, the devastating blow transforms into a gentle tap.

"Real funny, Tiny."

His eyes bulge in mock anger. "Tiny? You know what I should do to you for calling me that?"

"You won't do a thing, little fella."

Big Mike slams his fists into the bed and half yells, "Just wait until I put the Big back into Big Mike. You'll pay!"

He winces and looks ready to hurl.

"Still hurting, man?"

"Yeah. And the meds finished off what they started." Mike rubs his hand across the top of his head. It's no longer a dying wheat field. It's a barren land-scape, a pasty white bowling ball.

"Makes you look tough," I say. "One of your female admirers help with that?"

"I wish. Mom did it." Mike points at the box of comics. "Find any good ones in there? You should check out I Hate Fairyland. Pretty funny stuff. Done by one of my dad's friends."

Not wanting to tell Mike I'm not into fairy tales (classic novels with plenty of death and difficulty, please—and comics with fighting mice on occasion), I flip through the box, looking for the book he promises is "pretty funny."

Sandwiched between a stack of Archie & Pals and some vintage Batman is the book Mike wants me to investigate. I pull it from the pile. A green-haired maniacal young girl is on the cover, a gigantic bloody ax resting on her shoulder.

"Found the book," I say to Mike, whose eyes are already closed.

"It's good, man," he says, his voice easing into silence. His head rolls to the side.

With his closed-eye recommendation, I decide this is indeed a book I should check out. I wait a couple minutes to make sure Mike's good and out before sneaking out of his room with the comic.

I mouth a goodbye to his mom and raise the comic to let her know I'm taking it home to read. Mrs. Jackson moves toward me with silent speed, grabs my shoulders, and pulls me against her. Smells of deodorant and concern ooze from her. Try as I might to return the hug, she pins my arms to my side.

Four score and seven years later, Mrs. Jackson releases me, moments before suffocating me. She wipes her eyes and sucks up the emotional goo trying to escape her nose.

"Thank you, Adam." She says it with a soft laugh and another eye wipe. "Mike really likes having you around, and—" She sucks in a deep breath and lets it out all at once. "And things are a little brighter when you're here."

My long hair mashes against my cheeks, hiding the heat building there.

The walk home couldn't feel longer if it stretched the entire continent.

thirteen

Grandpa is watching Wheel of Fortune and eating off a TV tray.

"Trying to get in a win by playing without me?" I ask.

"Sit down and let your old grandfather show you how to play the game." Grandpa coughs and massages his throat with a pained look. He points at a TV tray beside the couch. "Yours," he says. "Start eating and get ready to lose to your roommate."

Somehow he beats me on the first puzzle. And the second. In the kitchen, Mom and Dad sound like they're talking to someone, but I don't hear a third voice.

"Somebody losing his magic touch?" Grandpa asks.

I chalk it up to the gorgeous pile of made-from-scratch macaroni and cheese in front of me.

I do a quick bit of catch-up and tie the game before the final buzzer. We solve the toss-up at the same time and head into the bonus round ready for anything when Mom and Dad stomp into the living room.

"Oh, hi, Shannon." Dad looks at Mom and then toward the kitchen. "You know Simon, don't you?" he asks.

Simon? I nod and feel my jaw scraping the ground. How'd the little squirt get in my house again?

"Had him over for dinner," Mom says. She rests her hand on Z's head. "He can eat his weight in mashed potatoes!"

Z holds a used Cool Whip container with mashed potatoes gurgling over the edges, which he clings to with chimpanzee fierceness. In an alternate universe, I send in armies of tens, hundreds, thousands, but none—not even the winners of the World's Strongest Man Competition—can pry that pile of potatoes from Z's grip. In the real universe, I raise an eyebrow as the mousy kid glides past and vanishes across the street.

I give Mom a what-was-that-about look.

She sighs and takes one of those stutter breaths that screams out, "Warning! Tears on the way!"

"Simon just—" she starts.

"Simon?"

"Yes, Simon," she repeats.

"But his name starts with a Z."

Mom finds something to stare at on the ground.

"We call him Z," I say, "so his name obviously begins with a Z. Maybe it's Zimon. Weird name, but it starts with the right letter."

Mom holds my hand, crushes it between both of hers.

"A long time ago, when Simon was little..." Mom looks at our hands, breathes deep. "Simon's dad..."

Ah, sheesh. Here we go again. Every time I turn around I'm stuck in some awkward situation where I don't belong. I fixed Mom and Dad's marriage, I practically landed Dad his new job (okay, not quite), Big Mike is fighting the world's deadliest disease, and now Mom's about to lay something at my feet heavier than Big Mike ever was.

I consider telling her to back off, to keep the adult stuff...well, adult stuff. I consider telling her I'm not mature enough to know what she's about to tell me. But I'm Adam Shannon Dakota Carr, and if there's one thing that I am, it's mature.

"He didn't want Simon. It was a bad, sad situation that hurt a lot of people. Drove Simon's mom to do a lot of things she's paying for now. And Simon..." Mom takes a stuttering breath. Dad nods verification to me. "He was only a newborn baby when it happened," Mom says, "but word travels when your dad doesn't want you around. Soon enough, kids started doing what they do. They turned the worst thing about Simon's life into his identity. They started calling Simon 'Z' because it's the last letter of the alphabet. They wanted to remind him that he was—according to his father—'the last thing anyone would ever want.'"

fourteen

Man-sized A's boxers push against Big Mike's window. I maneuver into my gray flip-flops when the smell of eggs grabs me by the nostrils. While I used to avoid breakfast at all costs, I'm going through something of a growth spurt. No, my concave chest isn't pointing in the right direction just yet and my arms are still thin as sausage links, but I'm getting a little taller. And that's kind of nice.

"Going somewhere?" Mom asks.

Not before I eat.

Belly full and brain awake, I skip across the street and give the front door a jolly rap.

"Hey, Z."

My mouth goes dry. My brain goes numb. Rendered mute, my left arm wraps around Z—Simon's shoulder.

Full of guilt, my mouth regains its strength. "Hi, Simon."

His shifty eyes indicate everything's normal. He scurries off, and I'm left to close the front door and track down a mask.

"Wondering when you'd get here!"

If Mike did any prep for my arrival, I can't tell. His boxers still hang in the blinds, and the same box of comic books sits by the chair. Beside the chair is a bedside table, a wadded paper towel full of Pop Tart crumbs where I left it days ago. (As an aside, this is yet another reason I wish my parents didn't think all-natural is the only way to go. Have you ever had a Pop Tart? Fresh out of the toaster or straight out of the box, they're one of the most delicious foods ever cooked up in a laboratory.)

The day passes with a little talking, some comic book reading while Mike sleeps, a peanut-butter-and-jelly sandwich, and more talking. When my stomach growls for the second time, I figure it's got to be dinnertime. Or close enough to sneak a bite of something Mom's busy cooking.

    "See you soon," Mike says.

    I wave a couple fingers good-bye.

fifteen

I'm chilling out in my bedroom as the smell of chicken smacks me in the face. But this chicken hasn't been prepared in the love-the-Earth-and-only-eat-things-the-way-Mother-Nature-says-to way. This chicken has been fried. Deep-fried.

I lick my chops like a rottweiler.

"Something smell good?"

"Uh—yeah, Mom."

She grins as Dad traipses into the kitchen.

He calls out greetings as Mom leans toward him. Dad obliges with a kiss, which activates my gag reflex. He hangs his coat across the back of the nearest chair and sniffs the air like a rabbit. "Is that…"

"It is," Mom says, "and before you get all excited, you should know it's not becoming commonplace around here."

A knock.

I look at Dad, who looks at me. We both look at Mom.

"Well, go answer it!" she says.

Dad and I race to the door. Dad draws his hand back and allows me the honor.

Mike, Mrs. Jackson, and Simon look hungry and well-masked.

"Come on in," Dad says.

Mrs. Jackson nods and thanks him.

Big Mike pushes his way through the door. Or rather, Simon pushes him through in a wheelchair.

As Mrs. Jackson watches, she holds out masks. Dad and I grab one, and Dad leads Mike's mom and Z to the kitchen.

"How'd you get over here?" I ask Mike. "I thought you were sick or something. You been faking?"

"Yeah," he says sarcastically. "I've been faking. Whatever it takes to get near that little nurse that can't keep her hands off me."

"Can't keep her hands off you?" I laugh.

"They're on you just long enough to jam another needle in your arm! And she's not been by in a long time. Starting to think she's given up on you."

Mike's nose catches something in the air.

"Whoa! Your mom made fried chicken? My favorite!"

And the mystery is solved. Mom didn't make fried chicken to please me. She didn't make it to please Dad. She didn't even make it to please Grandpa, who is sneezing and wheezing in the privacy of his bedroom. Nope. She made the fried chicken to please Michael Jackson, the one-time ogre from across the street who has morphed into a shell of a man-child.

I try to get upset with Mom, but fried chicken for any reason is cause for celebration.

Between bites, Mom, Dad, Mrs. Jackson, Mike, and I talk about everything that comes to mind. The main ingredient in the conversation is fried chicken, but Mike's health takes center stage as well.

Over and over, Mom comments on how good Mike looks—says his bald head will drive the ladies crazy. Mike responds with a head nod, guttural sounds meant to mimic the English form of "Thank you," or a smile with chicken pieces breaking through. Occasionally, he does all three at once—a sight to behold and an earful of disgusting sounds.

The only person not making a peep is—you guessed it—Simon. He's certainly eating, and he's using a fork and knife. But somehow he manages to make every move without a sound, even when slicing chicken from the bone on top of Mom's favorite China. When I realize his silence, I study him, waiting for a mistake in his technique—some sign that he, too, is human, that he can't achieve perfection with such an absurd task. But my gratification never comes. Not even a decibel of noise breaks free from his plate before Dad's voice brings me back to planet Carr.

"Shannon, you going to say bye?"

Mike and his mom are at the front door, their masks back in place after eating. I peer at Simon's chair. It's empty. He's beside Mike and Mrs. Jackson. Looks like he's been there the whole time.

sixteen

The rest of summer vacation is fairly dull. I read a few books—the Lord of the Rings trilogy for the third time, Ray Bradbury's Something Wicked This Way Comes, and Dan Wells' Partials, among others— hang out with Mike, go to a community pool with the lunch guys a couple times, and eat a lot of food that Simon likes and Mom makes. There is, however, one development worth mentioning.

I'm at Big Mike's, making fun of his sparse hair follicles and reminding him that my muscles are about to pass his in hugeness when my stomach growls. Mike's growled an eternity before, and Z—er…Simon was discharged to bring Mike something to eat.

Since I don't have a small, completely silent personal servant at my disposal—How do I get my hands on one of those?—I head home.

On the way out, I hear pots and pans simmering gently on the stove top. I stick my head in the Jacksons' kitchen to tell Mrs. Jackson goodbye. She's not there.

I jog across the street, pausing as Mike's mom steps out of my house. Her back is to me, and she talks to Mom, who is inside. Mrs. Jackson leans back in the house, and Mom wraps her arms around her. Stuck to Mom's face are what I saw for months on end last school year: tears.

When the two let go, Mrs. Jackson gives Mom a final goodbye. I wave to Mrs. Jackson as we pass.

The thought of getting involved in Mom's crying exhausts me, so I blow past her. I throw a "Hey, Mom" her way as I jet into the bathroom and close the door.

Grandpa gives a concerned look to Mom, who hasn't touched her food. "You okay?" he asks. "Don't like my daughter-in-law crying."

Mom puts down her fork, wipes her mouth like all the proper ladies do in all the proper magazines, and clears her throat. Dad freezes, a forkful of food in mid-air. Grandpa's gaze convinces Dad to hold off on the next bite.

"Simon's mother may be coming to live with them for a while," Mom says.

For the first time, I wonder about Simon's family. Who is Simon's mom, and why is she coming to stay with her son? Shouldn't he be with her already?

Instead of asking these questions and getting answers I'd rather not hear, I do what real men do when faced with tough questions: say nothing. My beloved tree-hugging mother, on the other hand, takes the opportunity to talk.

"She's—ummmm…she's had some hard times."

Dad and Grandpa give me gazes that say it's my turn to ask questions. Instead, I raise my eyebrows and throw my hands into the position known by humankind throughout time to indicate a lack of understanding.

"Simon's mom has made some bad decisions," Mom says, "but she is working really hard to—"

One, one-thousand.

Two, one-thousand.

Three, one-thousand.

"She's making better choices now," Dad says.

"She wants back in Simon's life."

I've heard enough. Scratch that. I've heard too much.

"Okay." It's a weak response, but it's all I've got. I've never read the manual on handling these situations. Probably won't write it any time soon, either.

seventeen

It's a new school year, and while pop music is all the rage, there is a growing love for rock and roll—which means my long hair won't stand out quite as much as it has in the past. But without Big Mike around to convince people that my long hair is the product of my love for all things rock and roll, I still stand out as the weirdo whose environmentalist parents won't let him get a trim.

Win some, lose some.

On the plus side, Noelle looks even finer than I remembered.

The lunch crew is back for another round of middle school. They spent every free moment in the summer playing video games, but I'm the one who has what everyone wants: news on Big Mike.

Is he still in military academy?
He never was.
Who'd he beat up to get kicked out?
He didn't beat up anyone.
Then why was he sent to alternative school?
He wasn't.
Where is he then?

The last one gets me. Do I tell them that Mike went nowhere more exciting than the hospital and his house? And if I do that, how much do I tell of his whereabouts and whyabouts?

When I hesitate to answer, the middle school crowd grumbles. They can't believe I was picked to be Mike's friend in the first place, and withholding information on who they assume is still the biggest and baddest creature in Palmetto Middle School's history is too much for them.

"Where is he then?"

"Yeah, where is he?"

"You sure you know anything about Big Mike?"

"I think you're making it all up!"

At lunch, the questions keep coming. They suspect that Mike moved, that I'm afraid to admit it because then no one would care about me. They want to know what Mike is doing or prove that I'm a fraud. Either one will satisfy.

I rub my neck and bow my head, letting my hair fall in front of my face. Would Big Mike care if I tell people what's going on? That he's been fighting death with poison? Is he worried about people thinking he's weak?

"He's at home."

I say it clearly, quietly. One particularly annoying kid with orange and white rubber bands stretched across his braces holds his hand to the crowd and leans toward me.

"He's what?"

The question silences the crowd.

"He's at home."

Disbelief sounds off in the forms of laughter and fake fart noises. I tuck my hair behind my ears and get up. Colored Braces Boy isn't having it though.

"He's at home? Doing what?"

The crowd quiets down again. How this kid can lead a herd of middle schoolers I'll never understand. Must be some special power in his braces. Maybe they act as antennae, tapping into the seventh grade mind. I picture him holding his braces high in the air to take over the entire middle school when his metallic voice breaks my vision to pieces.

"I said what's he doing—reading comic books or something?" He looks angry.

I snort.

"Yeah, he's reading comics," I say.

"Big Mike is reading comic books?" Mr. Braces huffs in disbelief.

"And dying of cancer."

Before my brain can react, my mouth pushes the words out. I look for the rewind button, the delete, the backspace. None are around.

Mike has cancer.

Everyone knows it.

All because of me.

Like that, I reduce Mike's fight for life to four stupid words. And I do it in front of middle schoolers who want Mike to fulfill their dreams of punching out kids in military academy. Kids who want to hear about Big Mike being Big Mike, doing Big Mike stuff—throwing boulders, eating razor blades, crushing adversaries. In an instant, I shrink larger-than-life Big Mike into small, weak Michael Jackson, lying in a hospital bed surrounded by nurses.

Big Mike is no more. All that's left is Mike.

I shove my hands in my pockets and push through the dumbfounded group.

eighteen

The cancer bomb rocks every corner of PMS. Hallways are quiet, teachers cautiously hug students, and the Goof Troop isn't pulling pranks on unsuspecting victims. They're being polite. They're being kind. They're smiling at me—sincere smiles that don't give away their next practical joke but tell me they're thankful a scrawny guy like me is caring for our school's most prized possession.

Life at home isn't nearly as calm. Almost every day, a little pipsqueak hangs out with my parents.

"Oh, hi, Adam!" Mom gets up from the kitchen table, where Simon holds a piece of bread. "Simon here needed a place to hang out for a few hours, so I made him my famous banana bread."

Okay, for those who forgot, Mom and Dad love planet Earth. A lot. So much that they try to avoid killing those sweet little cows that hang out in fields and chickens that are crammed in cages the size of Big Mike's head. And while a lot of their food tastes are a tad earthy for me, Mom's banana bread is manna from heaven.

I sit down and Simon's shoulders relax. Mom slides a sliver of banana happiness under my nose. I gingerly break off a bite and close my eyes in ecstasy, letting the flavors dash across my tongue. "So good," I mumble.

"Yeah."

An unfamiliar voice snaps me out of my breaded dream. My eyes open. No strangers are present. Just Mom and Simon, who is busy shoving another fistful of banana bread into his gaping mouth.

"So good," he says, repeating what the wise scholar known as Adam Shannon Dakota Carr said moments earlier.

"You can talk!" I say.

"Of course he can, Adam. What did you think? That he didn't know how?" Mom gives a look meant to turn a potentially tense situation into something harmless and even funny.

A high-pitched laugh makes me spin in my seat. I leap to my feet and eye a total stranger—a woman I've never, ever, ever seen, who laughs maniacally. Obviously she's escaped the loony bin and has come to find her next murder victim. Not gonna be me, though. Not with my—

"I'm Simon's mom."

My escape plan fizzles as I reach out to shake her extended hand.

"Sorry to startle you," she says. "Your mom invited me here. After all she's done for Simon, I had to meet her."

I hold back the temptation to inform Simon's mom that all my mom has done is give Simon the best pieces of banana bread…and the corner piece of lasagna…and made hamburgers just because he likes them. Instead, I squeeze out a compliment like the courteous young man that I am.

"She is something else, isn't she?"

And yes, she is something else. She gave me a girl name, forces me to keep my hair long, thinks Mother Nature ought to be a boy's best friend, and gave me a cell phone from 1999 with the power to call exactly one person: Mom. Or Dad. Or Grandpa.

Or whoever answers the phone at this two-bedroom bungalow.

"We should be going. Simon," his mother says, "we should take off. Need to help your aunt with dinner."

Simon, the boy formerly known as Z, and his mother, formerly known as the lady I'd never seen in my life but wound up inside my kitchen extending her hand to me as if it were some sort of formal interview—Wait, is she the one who honked at me while I stood dumbly and numbly in the middle of the road?—scurry from our house to help Mrs. Jackson with dinner.

nineteen

It's been a couple weeks since I ruined life for everyone at Palmetto Middle. Before I dropped cancer on each of their unsuspecting heads, they were concerned with voice changes, pimples, and sleepovers. None of that matters any more. Only cancer does.

Since I made the mess, I figure I should try to clean it up.

I leave my drab gray shirt at home and wear my "Be Like Mike" t-shirt. On the back, I attach a piece of customized art to cheer up my depressed classmates: a picture of Big Mike's big head. I'm not sure how long the double-sided tape will keep his massive mug in place, but it should stay on long enough to turn some frowns upside down.

Before the first bell sends students sprinting to homeroom, PMS is alive. I'd like to think it's the power of my clever shirt, but only a few people notice it. Granted, the ones who do are thrilled with its awesomeness. But most of the buzzing isn't about my t-shirt. It's about the fall dance.

I'm not sure why, but every sixth, seventh, and eighth grader in America thinks there is no option but to go to school dances. Only a few will actually take the option to dance. The rest will spend two hours scratching their backs against doorposts, laughing at the kids who are dancing, and eating soft mints that dissolve in the red, watered-down fruit punch served in tiny clear plastic cups. But they'll all go.

twenty

The theme of the fall dance is Under the Sea. John suggests I dye my hair aqua, Sam thinks I'd look good with a starfish-patterned vest, and Josh dares me to dress up like Aquaman.

Since I'd like to avoid getting beat up, I limit my aquamarine wear to a turquoise tie. Or something close.

"That's not even the right color!"

"Oh, you've got room to talk!" I point at Sam, who wears his daily, dirty tennis shoes and his every-other-day Minecraft t-shirt. I straighten my tie and give John and Josh a glance. They at least have the sense to wear dress pants and button-up shirts…even if they aren't tucked in.

"Didn't think anyone would notice," Sam says. "Little brighter in here than I expected."

I nod and shield my eyes. Most of the windows are blacked out, but the sun breaks through the large horizontal windows that the janitors decided were too high to bother with.

We creep to a corner, where there's less daylight to put our outfits on display. Unfortunately, the corner is already taken by Damien Childress and his ever-growing mustache. What started as a football team last year (eleven hairs on each side) has doubled in size, and his gaggle of female admirers has grown along with it.

"You girls know Shannon?" Mr. Mustache asks. He bows as if doing me some kindness.

I try thinking of a clever comeback, but all that comes to mind is the book I've been reading. I doubt a quip from Les Misérables will make sense to Mustache.

Thankfully, I'm saved by the music—or what passes as music these days. As the bass drops, my intestines rattle around like a rock inside a milk jug. I slither across the room, keeping the wall within arm's reach. John, Josh, and Sam follow.

We find an empty wall space and settle in.

"You see that kid trying to dance?"

"This music is about as good as the punch!"

"And I thought your outfit was bad…"

One-liners and self-conscious cut-downs flow freely. Then our group is invaded by the most gorgeous creature to walk the planet.

"Hey." It's only one word, but coming from Noelle, it transforms into a declaration of undying love.

As if on cue, my voice betrays me with a squeak, my "Hey" jumping a couple octaves above Noelle's. I clear my throat and start over, working to still my voice and play it cool. "Hey," I repeat in my suddenly deep, manly voice.

The music drowns out her next word. Thankfully, I'm a master lip reader, so I know exactly what she says: "Dance?"

I slowly follow her to foreign territory—the dance floor. Glance back at Josh, John, and Sam. They stare in awe.

A slow jam starts up. A love song.

Noelle rests her hands lightly on my shoulders. Mine are positioned stiffly above her hips. I'm in unchartered territory, but it has to be perfect. After all, our grandkids are going to beg for this story one day.

"That shirt is really cool."

"Thanks," I say, tucking my chin for a peek. "My mom ironed it."

Noelle speaks again, her angelic voice buried by a crooner singing, "Never, never, never…"

"What?" I almost yell.

"Not that shirt!"

She looks at me and I almost melt.

She looks at me and I do melt.

She looks at me and I re-congeal.

I shrug confusion with my re-congealed shoulders.

"The Mike shirt! The one with Big Mike's face on it!"

Noelle Kellogg, the Juliet to my Romeo, the jelly to my peanut butter, the backhand to my forehand, likes the shirt with Big Mike—the ogre whose real name is Michael Jackson—on the back.

For the next seventy seconds, Noelle and I rock back and forth from one foot to the other, making gradual movements that shift us in a tight circle. As we penguin, I wonder why she didn't say anything about the shirt earlier. It eats at me until Noelle asks if I'm okay.

I yell to be heard over the chorus that repeats

over and over. "Wish I knew you liked the shirt," I say. "Would have made you one!"

"Your best friend is Big Mike!"

I crinkle my brows. "Yeah?"

Noelle blinks.

"Big Mike! He's so popular!"

My heart scatters across the dance floor and gets stomped on by the entire middle school.

"You think being friends with Mike makes me popular? Look at me!" I tug at my long hair, gesture how much I hate it. I roll up my sleeves and show my puny arms, which have started to bulk up if I do say so myself. "And—"

The song ends. Silence engulfs the room. The perfect stage to finish yelling my sentence.

"I've got a girl's name!"

twenty-one

The first thing I see is Grandpa slipping on his shoes. I rub my eyes, let them adjust to the brightness, and walk into the living room. A massive pair of Athletics boxer shorts hang in Big Mike's window. I consider skipping breakfast, but it's Saturday and the growth spurt demands food. Mom and Dad are thankful. They push some eggs and a biscuit on me. Grandpa pipes up, says it's great I'm finally eating, that just maybe I'll get some muscles after all.

To this, I roll up my sleeves and flex, expecting the push-ups I pumped out after the dance to have some visible result.

"Looks about right for a fourth-grade girl,"

Grandpa says. He takes a bite of eggs and grins. "So you're looking better!"

He punches me on the arm playfully and winks to lessen the blow. Dad laughs a little. Mom grunts her disapproval. I try to scowl, but it's hard to get angry with the old guy.

The door pops open. Z—Simon stares at me with his wide-eyed stare. A little less scared than the past, but sheesh! Can't this kid learn how to be normal? I say, "Hey," and walk toward him. He moves to the side just before we collide. I slip on a blue mask.

Mike's passed out, and his puke bucket smells like bleach. Must have had a rough morning. I know he'll ask about last night, so I take advantage of his unconscious state to get my dance tale ready.

Mike yawns. "Hey, Adam."

I raise an index finger to finish the last three pages of a Batman comic.

Mike stretches in my peripheral vision, rubs his eyes, stretches again.

"Was I asleep?"

I show him my finger again.

"Adam!"

I hold up my finger firmly.

"Hey, man. Was I sleeping when you got here?" he asks again. "Sorry. Mom gave me something to ease the nausea. Guess it knocked me out."

I toss the comic book at him and flip up the footrest on my chair.

"Was I sleeping?" I ask mockingly. "Is the pope Catholic?"

Big Mike screws up his eyes, shakes his head, and changes the subject.

"How was the dance?"

"You wouldn't believe me if I told you."

"Oh, come on! You can't keep the good stuff from me! It's me—Mike, your bald-headed pal with the immune system of a newborn! I can't get out there, so you've got to share or I'm…I'm out of the loop! All I've got is this nurse back at the hospital who has the hots for me, and I don't think I should—"

"Okay, okay! I get it! I'll tell you about the dance." I hold my hands up to block whatever he plans to say next. "And unlike your story, mine is one hundred-percent true. But you're not going to believe it."

Mike looks like a forty-pound steak is just beyond his reach.

Time to feed the ogre.

I tell how Sam, John, and Josh watched in disbelief, their jaws scraping the food- and booger-encrusted cafeteria floor as my princess and I glided onto the dance floor. From here, I exaggerate the smoothness of my moves and finish the story with a flare.

"You did not!"

I eye him mischievously.

"Okay," I say, "I didn't kiss her. But I could have!"

Mike chokes on laughter and nearly falls off his bed.

"Michael Erwin Jackson, what are you doing?" Mrs. Jackson is white with worry. When Mike wipes away tears of laughter, she shakes her head.

"Since you feel so well," she says, "I'm stepping out of the house for a few minutes."

Mike is still recovering from my little lie when I tell him that Noelle mentioned him. He pulls himself to the edge of the bed.

"She what?"

"Yeah," I say. "She mentioned the one and only Big Mike."

"She's not even my type! Man, none of you guys at Palmetto Middle have a chance with the ladies, even when I'm sick in bed!" He pauses, soaks in his charm, kisses his formerly gigantic biceps through his mask. "What did she have to say about little old me?"

Big Mike is stunned. It's one thing to wear the shirt he gave me for my birthday. It's a totally different one to tape a picture of his face to the back of it.

"If you end up hitched, you've got me to thank, little man." Mike pats me on the shoulder. "Guess that makes me the best man."

I picture Noelle strolling down the church aisle, as I wait at the altar. Beside me stands a strangely dressed Sasquatch. His jacket sleeves are ripped off, the pant legs in shreds, the shirt buttons stressed to the point of popping. Big Mike. In a tux.

twenty-two

Mike's stronger today. I'm not sure if it's the image of me dancing with my dream girl that juices him up or if it's because his latest chemo treatment is wearing off. Whatever it is, he's animated—jumping around, imitating what he suspects I look like on the dance floor, re-enacting some of his finest fights at Palmetto Middle School, and even pretending to be Simon by standing in complete silence for days at a time.

At one point, I tell him his imitations are as good as his math skills. He punches me, and while it's not a full-blooded Big Mike punch, it has some kick.

"Least I don't share a room with my granddad!"

"Oh, come on! That's not even fair. Besides," I say, looking around the room at his hospital mementos, "not even Grandpa's spent as much time as you have in the hospital."

Mike sighs, shakes his head in agreement, runs his hand over his slick scalp.

I consider how much time Mike has spent in the hospital—a few weeks at the end of last school year and a few hours every couple weeks when he goes in for his chemo treatments. Realize I'm a jerk for mentioning it.

"Think I'm going to head home," I say. "Hang later?"

Mike's chest heaves. He collapses onto his bed and closes his eyes. "Yeah, I guess."

"You okay?"

"It's just that... Ah, never mind. It's stupid."

"And that's new?"

His mask pushes up to cover his cheeks as he smiles underneath. "It's dumb, but I'd do anything for some of those Lemonheads."

"The candy? I can go get you some."

"Or we could go together."

He's on the edge of his bed and scans the room, spots his house shoes, and slips them on.

"Great idea, champ, but I think—"

"This is no time for thinking, Shannon! Stop being such a girl. I'm feeling so much better. I've got to get out of the house. I'll wear this stupid mask, you can wear yours, and we'll be back in what—ten minutes?"

"Your mom would kill you!"

He holds out his hands to stop me from saying anything else.

"Hear that?" he asks. "Silence. There's nobody here. And that's who's gonna know about this. Let's go!"

His eyes sparkle with life, and I jog to catch up to him on the sidewalk. He moves with confidence, turning his head from left to right and back again, sniffing loudly through his mask in an attempt to smell the outside air.

He wears a t-shirt, pajama pants, and his red house shoes—drastically different from my overcoat, jeans, and sweater.

"Aren't you cold? Can't be more than forty degrees out here, man. It's freezing!"

"Feels good," he says. "Really good."

We get to the corner market and walk through to a loud dinging sound. A man who looks like he could use a good razor leans over the front counter, talking to a female customer. Both turn when we enter. Their eyes stay on us all the way down the candy aisle. The lady's eyes are wet and tired.

"You'd think they never saw a couple guys wearing blue masks or something," Mike says under his breath.

"Probably think we're gonna rob the joint," I joke.

Big Mike holds up a finger and pretends to shoot me with it. I catch the fake bullet in my hand and throw it back at Mike.

Before the repurposed ammo can hit its target, Mike looks down. "Last pack!"

He swipes the small Lemonheads box and takes off to the counter. As he approaches, the red-eyed girl steps aside. Mike tosses the box on the counter, and I reach for money to pay. As I hand the money over, the girl I thought had been crying opens her mouth and sprays a snotty sneeze across every nearby surface.

I look at Mike.

"Adam—we shouldn't be here..."

We rush back to Mike's house and wash our hands. I dump the Lemonheads into a bowl and set the candy on his bedside table.

"Never knew going to the corner store could be such an adventure," I say, "but I really do need to get home. You think you're okay?"

"My lady nurse friend may swing by to check in on me," Mike says, dismissing my question. "Just look for the boxers."

"Will do, Chief."

Mom and Dad talk in hushed tones.

"We can't fix everything," Mom says, "but we can do something."

Dad taps on the table, a rhythmic tapping that is his newfound calling card. He's not playing drums with his fingers. He's typing his thoughts on the table-top before saying them—a new trick he picked up as a legal writer.

The tabletop typing stops.

"Money?" Mom asks.

"Money," Dad says. "The treatment is working. They're just struggling to pay for it."

"It's not cheap," Mom admits.

"How much can we spare though? We're not exactly swimming in cash."

The two share a moment of thoughtful silence. When it's broken, they speak at once.

"We—"

Both stop.

Mom goes on.

"We have a healthy son," she says. "Julian's done what he can to help Mike. It took two weeks for Julian to recover, and he's trying to find a way to do more! We can help—even if it hurts."

My face burns. I creep to the front door and shimmy it open. I exhale, take a heavy step, and shut the door with authority.

"Mom, Dad—I'm home!"

I enter the kitchen to see Mom in a grimace. Dad eyeballs the table.

"What are you doing home, dear? Don't want to hang out with Michael any more today?"

"I'm hungry. Thought I should get some lunch."

Mom checks her watch.

"It is past one o'clock. Guess that's why I'm hungry, too." She jumps up and cracks open the cabinet, careful to keep her back to me. "Peanut butter okay?"

twenty-three

I hop off the bus and start toward PMS. A preppy eighth grader comes straight at me.

"Adam?"

We shake hands, my bitten-off nails only millimeters from his well-manicured ones.

"Yeah?"

"Sorry to bother you," he says, stuffing his hands in his khaki pockets. "Actually, sorry I've not introduced myself before."

This guy's got killer manners. As in I've-gone-to-one-of-those-super-weird-manner-schools manners. And he's one of the wealthier kids at school. At least I think he is. I've never seen him get off a bus—

so his parents must drive him every day. And he's not wearing a t-shirt. He's wearing a polo. Tucked in. He's either from a wealthy family, trying to look rich, or loony.

"I'm Othello."

I want to laugh, but hold back. His being in eighth grade and my having a girl name helps.

"Your dad works with my dad," Othello says. "At the firm."

"Whoa! What does your dad do there?"

Othello tilts his head and squints. "He's...he's an attorney—Julian Hart."

Why didn't Dad tell me his boss's kid is in eighth grade at Palmetto Middle? I could have had an older rich friend and dropped the video gamers.

"No way!" I reach my hand out for a second shake.

"Yeah," he says. "Just wanted to tell you I dig that shirt you wore the other day. The one with your friend on it—the big kid with cancer."

Cancer. The word is jarring. I release his hand. He shoves it back in his pocket.

I want to be upset. But Othello has a way with words, a sincerity. Besides, Mike does have cancer, and I'm the one who let the world know it.

"Thanks," I say. "He thought it was pretty great. Actually, he gave me the shirt for my birthday—kind of a joke, I guess."

Othello's nod says I gave more information than necessary.

"Anyway, I was thinking of doing something like you did. Think he would be cool with that?"

"You want a shirt with Big Mike's face on it?" I ask.

"Yeah. Don't think he'd be cool with the idea?"

I picture this well-dressed eighth grader in a t-shirt with Big Mike's mug plastered on the back.

"Yeah," I say. "He'd like it."

"Cool. Actually, I want to do something more than wear a shirt with his face on it."

Behind Othello, Josh smashes his face against a door window and sticks out his tongue. I wave to get him to stop, but it only encourages Sam and John to do the same.

Othello cranes his neck toward them.

"You need to go?"

"No, no, no," I say. "I'm good. I'd love to hear your idea."

twenty-four

My feet crunch in the February snow. Mike's boxers are always in the window these days, but they're not rooting on the A's. They're cheering for the Boston Red Sox. When I ask about the change, Mike says, "A guy's gotta win sometimes, right?"

I drop off my backpack at home, tell Grandpa and Mom good afternoon, eat a snack that Mom shoves in my face, and turn for Mike's house.

"Honey, wait."

I turn.

"Michael's not at home."

"Yeah he is," I say. "We've got a system."

Mom sighs and looks at Grandpa, who wipes

his nose.

"He caught an infection of some sort," Mom says. "The ambulance picked him up an hour ago."

Grandpa sneezes in agreement.

twenty-five

I tap on the door with my fingertips. Mike's dream nurse answers the door. Four million bobby pins keep her growing hair out of her face.

She points at the hand sanitizer. I get a squirt and rub it in.

"Just here to see Mike."

The nurse doesn't respond, and I mosey past her. Mrs. Jackson, Simon, and Simon's mom stand around the bed like they're at a funeral. Mike lies on the bed, assuming the position of a corpse: eyes closed, body stiff.

Simon and his mom slink out of the room.

"The doctor told me this could happen," Mrs.

Jackson says. She holds a tissue against her eyes and breathes in stuttering gulps.

I look at Mike with nothing to offer. No words for Mrs. Jackson. Because with all the heartbreak and death I've read about, I've never been trained in grief counseling.

Mike's barrel chest rises and falls almost imperceptibly.

"He's been getting so strong." Mrs. Jackson blows her nose. "He's put on so much weight." She coughs and whimpers. "He's been so…happy…"

She buries her face in her hands and leaves the hospital room to escape her son's sickness. I whisper an apology in her wake.

My legs shake. I collapse into the cushioned chair beside Mike's hospital bed and release every ounce of hurting oxygen stored in my lungs.

I flip up the footrest, lean back hard to force the chair into reclining position, drape my arms over my face. The monitors attached to Mike continue in a monotonous arrhythmia.

Beep.

Beep.

Beep.

AND I CHANGED THE WORLD

Beep.

Beebeep.

Beep.

An oxygen machine breathes steadily for Mike as if it has no concern in the world. But it sounds like Darth Vader. I don't know much about Star Wars—thanks, Mom and Dad—but I know he's the bad guy.

I sling my chair into an upright position. A pile of comics sits on Mike's bedside table. His mom must have thought he'd like having them nearby.

Grabbing the first book on the pile, I glare at the beeping and wheezing machinery around me. "Mike will beat you all."

With that, I read. Not to myself or for my own enjoyment. But to Mike, for his unconscious pleasure.

If you've never read a comic book out loud to someone, it's kind of tricky. Since most of the action takes place in pictures and the words are mostly what the characters are saying, making sense of a comic to someone with their eyes closed is borderline impossible.

But that doesn't stop me. I explain every picture and every detail, how the hero's facial expression clashes with his supposed confidence, and the person the hero plans to save looks like she'll be okay on her own. I give each character a unique voice. The hero, of course, has a deep, strong, confident voice, and the rescued person sounds a bit annoyed.

I read a couple hours. Fun as comic books are, reading them out loud this long is draining. The writing is witty enough, but it doesn't have the punch of Steinbeck or Hemingway. Maybe Mom's right.

For the first time, I look around the room. Hanging on the walls are three PMS football jerseys, each with names scribbled all over. They were given to Mike a few days ago, and now they serve as a needed sign of hope. I climb out of my chair and stretch my entire body at once.

"Care for a change of pace?" I ask unconscious Mike. "Thought you'd say that."

I grab the corners of the first shirt, scan the names scrawled all over it.

"Don't know any of these," I say, "but they're just little sixth graders. Seems only yesterday that was us, down at the bottom of the middle school barrel."

I move to the seventh-grade jersey—the one with the names I know by heart. I twist it until I find a name I want to read out loud. One that will get Mike's attention.

"Ah, here we go. Looks like my three best buds all signed together." I look at Mike, hoping for some kind of reaction out of him, hoping he'll wake up and be fuming mad that someone has taken his position as best friend. But he doesn't flinch.

I say their names slowly, letting each have time to break through Mike's subconscious. "John Garner." No response from Mike. "Sam Clove." Not a movement or sound. "Josh Crew." Nothing.

I scan for more names with some meaning behind them. There's Damien, who signed his name clearly, a confident, thick mustache drawn below as a visual aid to his identity. Mike's football buddies all signed where Mike's kidneys would be, a poorly drawn football surrounding the signatures. I read the names, one at a time. The only response is electronic breathing and beeping.

Finally, I flip the shirt over. I read a few random names and gasp. There, in perfect feminine penmanship, is the name that has set my heart racing since my first step inside PMS. My mouth goes dry.

"Found a good one," I say to Mike's hospital room. "You ready?" I give a sly grin to the still sleeping Mike. "You can probably guess who it is, but I'll tell you anyway. Noelle Kellogg, the finest chica in the galaxy."

I stand spellbound by her handwriting. Is this love?

I relive our dance routine as the rhythm of Mike's attached beeps morphs into a nonstop ringing sound. Before its meaning registers in my brain, Mike's mom and nurse are in the room.

The nurse's look tells me to scram and coincides with a sharp jerk from Mike's mom. The incessant beeeeeeeeep screams at me as I stand outside Mike's room.

Mike's mom falls to her knees beside Mike's bed, grabs his hand, presses her forehead against the bed. The nurse shoves a needle into Mike and holds two fingers against his throat while counting. Mrs. Jackson and the nurse look up at me and yell. Both look at me and yell again. They look at each other in frustration and then at me. They yell—a third time. This time, my ears work.

"Move!"

I get out of the doorway just before a team of doctors mows me over.

twenty-six

Spanish class with Señor Walch is exhilarating, but not for me—not today. None of the lesson breaks past the image swirling in my head of Mike lying peacefully, his eyes shut with finality.

The crack of the intercom system breaks through my zoned-out brain.

"Adam Carr, please come to the front office. Adam Carr, to the front office."

I'm almost out the door when Sr. Walch stops me.

"Toma tu mochila."

Perfect time for Spanish practice, Sr. Walch.

"Your bag," he says with a deflated Spanish accent. "You should probably take your bookbag in case you don't come back."

Backpack across my shoulder, I slug down the hall to the office. Mom pushes out of a chair.

"Michael's going to be okay," she says. "He wants to see you."

The elevator opens, and I hear Mike's voice. It's weak and slow, but it's definitely him. I toss on a surgical mask and enter.

"The dead walk," Mike jokes. "Or lie in hospital beds talking."

In just a few minutes, Mike's spirit and vocal chords regain their strength. He yells stories and guffaws at everything I say. The only time he grows quiet is when he asks how the love of his life—the blonde nurse—has taken his hardship.

"She was heartbroken—crying, freaking out," I say. "You know women." Mike's chest swells beyond capacity. "Fortunately," I say, "I was there to comfort her."

Mike throws a half-hearted air punch at me.

"Better not mess with my woman!" he says. "I'll tell Noelle! And don't think I won't!"

I try to figure out how Mike will tell Noelle anything. He's got enough hoses running out of him to be a stunt double for Doc Ock, but I don't tell him that. After all, he's in the middle of beating cancer into the ground. No reason he couldn't find a way to send a message to a middle school damsel from his hospital room.

"Yes, sir!" I say with a salute.

His nurse walks in and I give a mischievous look. Mike shakes his head, silently begging me not to embarrass him.

The hospital visit ends, and I crash hard at home.

"Well done, Adam!"

Grandpa lies on his side. His covers are bunched up against him, and both his aged feet hang off his twin mattress.

"Well done?" I ask, wiping away eye boogers. "What did I do?"

"Slept 'til almost eight o'clock—something I could never do at your age."

I roll my eyes and know what's coming next: a lecture about how Grandpa couldn't sleep in that late when he was my age. His life didn't let him. Cows had to be milked and younger siblings tended to.

I've tried to explain that it's not my fault Grandpa was raised in the boonies on a tiny farm with a huge family, but it didn't convince him the first time, so I don't bother any more. Instead, I take a different approach.

"Oh no! What's happened?" I open my eyes as wide as possible. "Am I on a farm, Grandpa? Is this 1902? Where am I?"

"Very funny, Adam Shannon Dakota Carr," he says through a cough. "But I need you to do something for me." He looks away and sneezes, waits for a second sneeze that doesn't come, reaches toward me with his pointer finger. "Pull that, if you don't mind."

I get to my feet and grab hold, just as a monstrous sound bounces off the walls. A hidcous smell fills the room.

"Grandpa!"

He gives an old-man chuckle. "And wash your hands. Your mother thought I had a cold before, but it's starting to feel like the flu. No need you getting sick, too, roomie."

twenty-seven

I escape the stench to be met by the sweet smell of pancakes and bacon. A disheveled blanket on the couch sends me back to last year, when Dad slept there for weeks on end. My stomach swirls until I see him. I relax. It's not Dad.

"Simon?"

He holds a forkful of pancake inside his open mouth, frozen in place. Maybe he's waiting for me to grant him permission to bite. Or maybe he's just a weird kid.

Whatever causes it, the trance breaks when Mom gives her version of abracadabra: "Good morning, Shannon."

"Morning," I echo. "Simon?"

"You look like you've never seen him before," Mom says. "It's just Simon. Or as we like to call him—Z."

Z? Didn't Mom tell me not to call him that? That it's demeaning, a reminder that his dad doesn't want him around?

I shake my head and sit across from Si—Z and fill my plate with oval-shaped pancakes. Z stares at me. His eyes bore through my skull, which holds one of the most precious gifts to the human species: my brain.

"Got enough, son?"

I lower the syrup. My plate swims in the stuff.

Dad leans against the kitchen doorway.

"Think that should do you for a week or two," he says. "Make that a month or two."

I suck air between my front teeth and grab my fork and knife, careful not to drip syrup onto the table.

"I...I like 'em this way." My first bite has a never-ending syrup tail that's still attached to the plate when I bite down. Z—Simon—Z?—sniggers, covers his mouth, turns red.

Mom hugs Z below the green owl clock that

hangs over the front door.

"Bye-bye, Z. See you tonight."

She closes the door, peeks through the window at him.

"Z?"

"What can I say?" Mom shrugs. "He likes the name. Said Simon felt weird. So we're back to Z."

"But what about..."

"Z says he doesn't care why he got the name or any of that. I told him we could change the meaning if he wanted. He's usually the last person to say something, so the name fits."

I brainstorm reasons Z would speak before anyone else, but none come to mind. I picture a volcano erupting, spewing lava all over him. He waits for everyone else to yell, "Run!" before making a peep. Someone hands him a check for a million bucks. But even then, he waits to learn why the check was given to him before saying, "Thank you."

"Guess it works," I say. "And did you say you'd see him again tonight?"

Mom yanks the crumpled blanket off the couch and motions for me to grab the other end. "He needs a place to stay for a few nights," she says. "With Mike in the hospital and Z's mom—"

Mom looks down, focusing hard on the task at hand.

"His mom?" I ask, trying to hide my interest.

"She—she's still not doing well." Mom clears her throat and regains her composure. "So with her not around right now and Mike's mom at the hospital most of the time, your father and I offered to have Z stay here a few nights. Until everything can get back to normal."

We make the final fold, and I hand my half to Mom. She pops open the closet and sets the blanket on a shelf.

"Catch!"

Dad sends Z's pillow from last night soaring toward Mom's head. She reaches to grab it, but she's too slow. The pillow smacks her face.

Dad jogs around the couch and grabs Mom by the shoulders.

"You okay, Carol? Didn't mean to bop you there."

Mom nods and chuckles.

"So I come by my athletic prowess honestly."

Mom waves away my comment. "Adam, you may not be a prized athlete, but you're special in your very own way."

"Special in my own way?" I ask. "Just what every middle school guy wants his mom to say."

It's the first Monday in April, and two bowls of oatmeal are on the table when I get home from school.

"Have to eat early, honey." Mom grimaces. "Grandpa is in the hospital. We're going to eat real quick and—"

"Grandpa's in the hospital?" I drop into a seat.

"He should be fine, dear. Just struggling to get over that flu. Doctors say it turned into pneumonia." She tilts her head to determine if I pick up on the worry she accidentally broadcasts across the table.

My response: avert eyes to bowl of oatmeal and begin eating.

The oatmeal is—well, it's oatmeal. I slurp it down, run to my room, and grab Grandpa's class ring. I'm back in the kitchen before Mom finishes her food.

"Mom, let's go!"

I twist the ring in place on my index finger. Mom bends over her bowl for another bite, wipes her mouth carelessly with her hand, and we're off.

twenty-eight

A light green curtain splits room 113 in half. The television runs wide open on one side. Grandpa's half is quiet.

"Hey, Shannon," Dad says. He stands to hug me and nods at Grandpa, who looks in pain. "He's sleeping right now. Been a rough day, but the doctors say he should be okay."

There are only two chairs, so I stand. I shift from one leg to the other when the pain and stiffness gets intolerable. Mom offers me her chair, and Dad does the same. I'm a man, though. I don't need to rest.

When the clock on the wall reads seven o'clock, a nurse cuts through the curtain to check Grandpa's vitals.

She rests her fingers on Grandpa's wrist and watches the second hand on the clock over Grandpa's bed tick by one second at a time. Her movements are practiced and effortless. She slips a stethoscope beneath Grandpa's hospital gown, writes on her clipboard, feels his forehead and cheek.

Quick as she arrived, she disappears through the curtain wall. When she reappears, she's got a chair for me.

I thank her and wonder if Big Mike would fall for this one, too. She's a bit older, has a few extra pounds around her midsection, and wears a wedding ring. Guess that's a no.

I settle into the armed chair. My legs thank me for the much-needed break, and I stretch my back, letting my arms and legs extend straight in front of me. After half an hour of small talk I hear a faint, familiar song drift through the room.

"Jeopardy!"

I hop out of my seat and feel the right side, left side, and then the bottom of the flat-screen television hanging in front of the curtain. The contestants are already on the third answer. It's a tough one. I reach over and tap Grandpa's arm.

"Game time, Grandpa. It's okay if you sleep through it, though. You'd probably lose anyway. And be glad we missed Wheel of Fortune. Would have been a rough one for you."

With that, it's game on. There's only one guy who is man enough to pull off the victory, and that guy is—

"What is beeswax?"

I look at Dad as the television contestant echoes Dad's question.

"You may beat Grandpa," Dad says, "but you've never gone against me."

"Ahem?"

"Or your mother," Dad says with a sigh. "Yes, Carol, you are welcome to play as well, if you want. But be warned," he says, "this is a man's game."

Mom: "Who is Andy Griffith?"

Dad: "What is 1884?"

Mom: "What is 'Who Framed Roger Rabbit?'"

Me: "Who is Mickey Mouse?"

Me: "What is a dale?"

We're pretty close to tied and agree that the Final Jeopardy question will settle the matter. Mom and I get it at the same time, leaving Dad to claim last place.

He groans to his feet, stretches, looks at his watch.

"Should probably go," he says. "Visiting hours are just about over."

We file past Grandpa, his breathing quiet and irregular. Mom kisses Grandpa's forehead and I peck his cheek. Dad's eyes swell, and his chest heaves as he bends over his own father.

I move toward the exit. Grandpa's nurse looks up from her computer screen and whispers, "Good night."

I push through the double doors, go a few paces, and stop at the waiting room entrance. I lean against the large glass wall framing the room and wonder how Z and his mom are doing. She picked him up from our house a few days ago and rushed away like she was kidnapping him. If there was ever a time to look scared, that was it. But somehow, Z looked at ease.

The double doors creak open to reveal Mom and Dad walking hand in hand—Dad wiping his eyes, Mom taking breaths straight out of those how-to-breathe-when-you're-having-a-baby classes.

At home, I wonder if I'll be able to fall asleep without the sound of Grandpa snoring to push me into la-la land. It's weird, but I've grown to love his annoying chainsaw going on and off, off and on as I sleep. Grown to need it, even.

Fortunately, my fears of not being able to fall asleep are unfounded.

"No, no, no…no, no…"

In my dream, a voice repeats it over and over. The voice says it two, three, four, five times in close repetition, followed by a breath. Then the refrain continues: "No…no, no…"

"Adam, Adam!" Mom sits on the edge of my bed, her face stained. "Shannon, wake up, sweetie. Adam, wake up. I'm so sorry. I'm so sorry…"

In the other room, Dad says "No" over and over like a broken record.

"Mom? Is Grandpa…?"

Mom bites her lip and falls into my shoulder. Her body heaves.

"Yes," she says between sobs. "Yes…"

twenty-nine

White shirt, black tie, khakis. Not my normal everyday wear. But it's what you wear to these things.

I fake a smile as well-meaning person after well-meaning person filters through the church and tells me what a great man my grandfather was. As if I don't know it. As if he wasn't my favorite person in the world, the only person I ever wanted to go against in Wheel Of Fortune and Jeopardy. The only person whose erratic breathing and snoring became the soundtrack of my life. The only person who saved my world when I thought I was saving my parents' marriage.

I know Grandpa was a great man. And all I

want is for him to be here, to laugh at life, to punch me in the arm when yet another person compliments his great personality. But it's not happening. And if there's any doubt, the impending trip to the graveyard will remove it.

I'm worn out from head-nodding and the never-ending line of people telling their favorite stories of Grandpa. Then Big Mike, Mrs. Jackson, and Z reach the front of the line.

"Hey, man." Big Mike breathes deep, shakes his head, and reaches up from his wheelchair. I lean down and he pulls me in for a death-defying bear hug. He squeezes until my spine shivers. One, one-thousand, two, one-thousand. Release. Mike looks at me and then at the ground, wipes his eyes. He breathes loudly through his mask.

"Oh, Adam, I'm so sorry for your loss." Mrs. Jackson's arms—exceptionally thin and frail after being wrapped in Mike's—squeeze even tighter. "I'm so sorry," she repeats as she backs away and moves on to my parents.

"Mrs. Jackson?"

Mike's mom steps back toward me, smiles in sympathy.

"Yes, Adam?"

I breathe in every ounce of courage available. "It was my fault—Mike going to the hospital. I did it. He wanted some candy so we went to the corner store and there was this lady there who I thought was all sad but she was really just sick with the flu or something and I know that's where Mike got that bug that sent him to the hospital." The words sprint out of me, thankful to escape and get out in the open.

Mrs. Jackson puts a hand on my cheek. "Adam, it's not your fault."

"But I—"

"Adam, I've known about that trip you two made since the day you made it. Michael getting sick isn't your fault, Adam. What is your fault," she says looking at Mike, "is that he's getting better."

She wipes a tear from my face and kisses my forehead. When she steps toward Mom and Dad, I'm faced with Z. But not for long. Z steps back, and someone steps in front of him.

"Hi, Adam," she says. "I'm sorry about your grandpa. Sounds like a really nice guy. Z liked him a lot."

It's Z's mom. She's put on a few pounds, her eyes are bright, and her hug is gentle and genuine. I thank her and wave to Z as they move on.

Big Mike stays put.

"Hey, man," he says, repeating the only words he said before. "I'm sorry... I really liked your grandpa. He was—he was like a granddad to me. Sorry..."

My vision blurs. Dad grabs me from the side.

After shaking forty-six million hands, I wash my own a few times before climbing into bed in the galaxy's loneliest bedroom.

Grandpa's smell is all over the place. I settle into the covers. Hear his sheets rustle. Strain to hear his familiar snoring. A sound catches my ear. I strain to hear it better. But it's just a memory.

I flip from my right to my left to my right to my stomach to my left to my back, looking for sleep with every turn. All that meets me is life without Grandpa.

I turn on the light and grab a pen and paper.

According to Better Homes and Gardens—or maybe it was Oprah magazine—if you're having a hard time sleeping, you should write your ideas down. Gets them out of your head and onto a piece of paper, so you can be done with them and move on to the sweet world of sleep.

I spin the pen in my hand, push the paper back and forth across the bedside table, and write the first thing that comes to mind.

I remember you used to say I was your pride and joy. And man, I wish you could stay, but I know you're going to a better place.
I love you, Grandpa.

thirty

The PMS student body walks as a loose herd across the street and into the high school auditorium.

We've had a couple assemblies this year, but this is the first time anyone wants to go. Kind of hard to get stoked over the first-of-the-year make-it-the-best-school-year-ever speeches from the principal and teachers. Even harder to skip across the street when you know you're being served a two-hour discussion on why we need to work a little bit harder at math and science and "Don't you remember the talk at the beginning of the year when we were all excited to make this the best school year yet?"

Row by row, the auditorium fills up with sixth,

seventh, and eighth grade students. Along with them come sounds and scents that mimic those of the Palmetto Zoo.

Othello stands onstage alongside Vice Principal Confetti, The Glowing Orb, Principal Horton, and a couple eighth-grade teachers I don't know by name. He scans the crowd, waving and smiling to his friends. When he spies me, Othello motions for me to come to the stage.

I salute my teacher, point toward the stage, and head toward Othello. The content of my cargo pants bangs heavily against my left leg as I skip up the steps and onto the stage.

"Hey man, cool that you're here."

Yeah, it is cool that I'm here. And I love that Othello recognizes that.

"Cool that you're doing this," I say.

A quick glance lets me know I took his word. Othello lets ring a solo "Cool" to reclaim it as his own.

I scope out the crowd from the stage. Clusters of like-dressed and similar-talking middle schoolers have their heads inches from one another to hear over the noise. I keep looking, hoping to find a few friendly faces to wave to and up my cool factor. The only people looking back are the video game boys. But they're my only social connection at PMS these days, so I grin and lift my index and middle fingers toward them like a mafia boss.

Mom and Dad walk through the back of the auditorium and take a seat. Dad's tie is loose. His shirt sleeves are rolled up and hang free from his elbows. Mom isn't substitute teaching today, but she wears her substitute teacher getup out of habit.

"Time to settle down in here," Mr. Confetti says, his voice almost inaudible despite the microphone. He jumps in the air and taps his loafers together. No one seems to notice.

"Tough crowd," he says into the microphone. Still no response. "This thing on?"

Mr. Confetti brushes his hair with his hand, leans back to eye the stage hands, and points downward. The house lights dim and everyone quiets down. The near silence, however, isn't enough for Mr. Confetti.

A few moments of stifling laughter and shuffling feet, and the silence is complete.

"Thank you," Vice Principal Confetti says. "I knew you could do it."

After a dramatic pause—the type that adults rely on to let jokes sink in and crash to the floor—he continues.

"This is a unique day. A day that will be remembered in the Palmetto Middle School hallways for decades." He pulls a blue mask from his pocket and slips it over his mouth and nose. Everyone in the auditorium straps on their own masks. Then Vice Principal Confetti holds out his right arm and steps away from the microphone.

The entire auditorium of middle school students—the same students who can't sit still for their annual booster shots—sit absolutely still, most holding their breath.

A moment passes.

Another.

One more for good measure—or is it torture?

Then, a step. A heavy step. A step that could only be made by some sort of monster. A larger-than-human creature that could eat every ounce of food in the school cafeteria if given the chance.

thirty-one

A spotlight steadies on the right side of the stage. Into it steps a being that was once the most feared creature at PMS. He's lost his hair and some muscle mass and he dons a blue surgical mask. But he's still Big Mike.

The auditorium goes nuts. There's cheering, clapping, yelling, screaming, whistling, and every other type of man-made noise you can imagine.

Mike makes his way across the stage. He pauses, takes in the scene, pulls his mask slightly away from his mouth, and lets it pop dramatically back into place. He wipes his eyes, but there are no tears. They can't be. Mike's back at PMS, where he is king. And kings don't cry.

I'm not sure how long he stands in the center of the stage before Mr. Confetti scoots up to the microphone and yells into it: "Big Mike!"—a simple message that sends the crowd into a renewed frenzy, as if Mr. Confetti's admission confirms what everyone suspects but is unsure of—that this is indeed their beloved Michael Jackson, their very own Big Mike.

Chills cover my spine. I try to hoot and holler, but some feelings try to get out at the same time. So I swallow and slap my hands together.

Eventually, the crowd dies down. Othello holds the microphone. He eyes Big Mike and shakes his head.

"Man, it's good to have you here," Othello says through a mask. A handful of hoots and hollers break out in the crowd in approval. "Real cool you could come."

Mike shakes his head and bends at the waist so his bald head faces the crowd. He swipes his hand back and forth over his head. Cheers are followed by uncomfortable quiet.

Othello isn't phased.

"You probably don't know me," Othello says, "but I know someone you do know. Shannon?"

I walk toward Othello, realizing he called me by my girl name in front of the entire school, yet the world didn't crumble.

Mike sticks out his fist for a power bump. Our hands explode and return to their former states—his the size of a waffle iron, mine closer to a thimble.

Othello passes the microphone to me and mouths, "It's all yours."

I fumble the microphone, and it slams against the stage. A giant thud roars through the auditorium, followed by a pile of feedback that grows to painful proportions. I pick up the microphone and hold it overhead, as the student body covers their ears.

The feedback subsides.

"Sorry about that," I say.

The crowd grows ten-fold as my face burns. Breathe, Adam. Breathe!

"Welcome back, Mike," I start. "It's good to have you here." The whole of PMS shakes in agreement. "I'm, uhhh…I—I'm not sure how to say this, so I'll just make it happen, I guess. Lights!"

thirty-two

The spotlight disappears and the whole place goes black. A rustling passes through the sixth grade, the seventh grade, the eighth grade, the teachers, the maintenance crew.

Then every light in the place flickers on at full blast. The entire audience stands, every other person standing backward and every other facing forward. They all wear a shirt that reads "Be Like Mike" on the front with a picture of his massive face on the back.

I lift the mic to my mouth: "Mi-ike! Mi-ike!"

The auditorium catches on and begins yelling his name in unison. The chant rumbles the stage underfoot. Mike's mom stands behind the stage curtains, tears pouring from her face.

Mike takes a deep breath and raises his right hand to the crowd.

I approach the microphone again, but can't speak. It feels like a toothpick is stuck in my throat and nothing, especially not a word, is getting past it.

So I pull an envelope out of my back pocket and pass it to Mike without a word. He opens it to my encouragement.

For a moment—a split second—Mike looks ready to pass out. His knees buckle and he stumbles backward. When he catches himself, he waves his mom over. By the time she's to his side, Mike is cross-legged on the stage floor.

Mrs. Jackson takes a knee and grabs Mike for the firmest hug in middle school history. Amazingly, Mike doesn't disintegrate in a heap of embarrassment. Then again, this is Big Mike—the guy no one can hurt, even when he's lost half his muscle mass and all of his hair.

Mike holds his mom longer than any middle schooler should. They release, and he leaps to his feet. The crowd gasps as Mike breaks into the worst moonwalk ever performed.

Doubled over with laughter, I gaze at the crowd,

where the most glorious creature on Earth laughs through tears.

"You guys are crazy!" Mike yells into the microphone, pointing across the audience. "Crazy! Fifty thousand dollars worth of crazy!"

Othello gives me a knowing smile and raises his hands in the air. His right hand holds all five fingers up and the left is formed in a zero to indicate that yes, the check inside that envelope is worth fifty thousand dollars.

In the rear of the auditorium, my parents hold up their hands like Othello—fifty thousand dollars! The crowd raises their hands in the same way and starts chanting again: "Mi-ike! Mi-ike!"

I slip backstage to grab a chair and an extension cord. Place the chair to the right of the microphone stand and have a seat. Remove a pair of scissors from my side pocket and motion to Big Mike.

"Cut it!" I yell into his ear.

"What are you doing?" he yells back.

"Cut it!"

Big Mike swipes the scissors from my hands with gusto and raises them in the air.

"Mi-ike! Mi-ike!"

With the first scissor stroke, the volume exceeds

that of a sonic boom. A fistful of hair plunges to the stage, the soft sound buried deep beneath the frantic auditorium. Another handful of hair and then another fall, one after another. Finally, the bulk of my hair is no longer attached to my head.

"You look like a butchered Chia Pet!" Mike yells into my ear. "It looks hilarious!"

"You're not done!"

I snatch clippers out of my pocket and hand them to Mike. He plugs them into the extension cord and gets going. As he cuts, the chanting continues and begins to moves toward the stage. By the time Mike shaves my head as close to bald as it's going to get, a line of middle school students snakes down the stage, around the right aisle, along the back wall of the auditorium, and down the left aisle, stopping just short of the stage.

The chanting morphs into general applause, hooting, and hollering. Kids run around high-fiving everything in sight. A few high-five the air. Noelle isn't crying any more. She stands where she's been for the last fifteen minutes, her hands slapping together mindlessly.

I strut to the front of the stage to give everyone a good look at my new do. When I rub my head, Noelle waves. I wave back confidently.

thirty-three

It takes two hours to shave everyone's hair in line. All said and done, nearly one-third of the male PMS student body and at least a dozen females stand in line waiting to shave their heads. Most see it through to the end. A handful of parents come prepared with clippers, brooms, and dustpans to help.

As the line dwindles, I grab Othello.

"Fifty thousand dollars?" I ask. "I mean, I gave my lawn-mowing money, but it wasn't that much. And everyone out there had a shirt! I thought there were kids who didn't buy one."

"Yeah," he says. "Big Mike's a cool guy. Dad wanted to help, so…"

"So he gave fifty thousand dollars?"

I try to comprehend what that much money would look like in a duffle bag. Sure, his dad is a lawyer, but fifty thousand clams? For a kid he doesn't even know?

"It wasn't exactly fifty thousand dollars," Othello says. "We raised almost ten thousand in shirt sales and donations."

"Fifty thousand dollars…" I whisper it to myself, as I imagine shoving every dollar into an imaginary duffle bag.

In a daze, I follow Othello to Mike, who sits with his mom at the rear of the stage. Othello bends down to Mike's level.

"Very cool day," Othello says. "Dad wanted to be here, but—"

"But nothing!" Mike says. "Your dad is the only reason I'm here!"

Big Mike turns to me, giant tears in his eyes.

"Adam," he says, "do you know what Mr. Hart did for me?"

Mrs. Jackson wraps an arm around her son, her eyes full of smaller tears.

I shake my head. "Fifty thousand dollars…"

Big Mike pinches his eyes shut. "He…" Mike

sucks in a breath and holds it. "He donated bone marrow to me, Adam. Doctors said if I didn't get a bone marrow transplant, I'd have been a goner."

Mrs. Jackson bites her lips then stands and wraps her arms around Othello.

School's a lost cause for the rest of the day. All anyone can talk about is Big Mike, shaved heads, and fifty thousand dollars. The only thing I can think about is bone marrow.

The guys who shaved their heads rub them for good luck. The girls who shaved their heads sit in fear, wondering if their parents will be upset. The girls who like the guys who shaved their heads ask to touch the prickly tops just to be near the guys and part of history. The guys who like the newly bald girls tell them not to sweat their parents' response. And the guys who didn't shave their heads? They're out of luck.

Mustache takes this particularly hard. Having spent his entire life growing his mustache to get the attention of the ladies, he now sits alone at his desk, disheartened at his full-head-of-hair and upper-lip-of-hair fortune.

thirty-four

I should have been more concerned about Mustache's feelings.

"Thought I'd go above and beyond," he says to a group gathered around him.

I can't get a good visual, but I can tell he got rid of his hair. Not sure what's above or beyond about that, but if he's willing to support Big Mike—even if it's a couple days late—more power to him.

"You see Damien, the kid with the mustache?"

I turn and tell Josh that yeah, I know he shaved his head. "Glad he did it," I say.

Josh leans close. "Yeah, he shaved his head. But did you see him? Looks like something out of a sci-fi flick—an alien that didn't eat his vitamins or some-thing."

I shrug. Bald doesn't do much for me either. Maybe my parents were right to keep my dome cov-ered.

"We all look pretty weird," I say. "Seen yourself lately?"

Sam and John yell, "Burn!"

The bell rings, and we go our separate ways.

As I dodge students scurrying to class, I see Mustache, a.k.a. Damien. With just a glance, I realize Josh is right. The kid looks weird. Really weird. Weird enough that it's hard to look at him. Even harder to look away. And he walks right up to me.

"Hey, man," he says. "Thought I should shave my head, too."

I eyeball Mustache, trying to figure out what makes him look so much stranger than the rest of us.

"Decided to do a little more, too," he says. "Got rid of the eyebrows."

It's like Mustache has two white hyphens above his eyes, slits on his forehead the sun has never touched. No wonder no one can look the kid in the eyes. But I have to try.

"You sure did," I say cautiously. "Still have the

mustache though."

He takes two fingers and spreads the mustache out to its fullest potential. There isn't much potential there, but I don't tell him that. He's already missing his eyebrows. No need to take his false sense of pride, too.

"Considered chopping it off," he admits, "but I had to draw the line somewhere, right? Kind of my calling card now. How the ladies know I'm a real man."

I swallow hard and give thanks that class is starting.

thirty-five

It's only been a few weeks, but some people's hair has grown out so much it looks like it wasn't shaved in the first place. Mine seems upset to have been cut and fights against growing back.

I'm in Ms. Short's class. Barely taller than the shortest seventh grader (that's Bill Landrum, whose head slams into people's stomachs), Ms. Short's hair is cropped tight, and her mouth is permanently pursed in reflection of her short temper. I listen as she talks about whatever seventh grade math teachers talk about. Okay, I'm not listening. I'm pretty sure I know everything she's taught, because I've not listened a day this year and I've made perfect grades the whole time.

I slide low into my desk chair, cross my arms, and lean my head back to count the pencils hanging from the ceiling tiles.

Ms. Short's door creaks open, but I don't look up. There are still more pencils to count.

I'm so focused that I don't budge when my name is called or when the class goes uncharacteristically quiet. Then a meaty hand waves in front of my face.

I jerk to the side and look up. Looming in front of me is a gigantic creature with a backpack slung across its shoulder and a blue surgical mask across its face.

"Mike!"

"Was wondering if you'd ever see me!"

I jump up and almost lose my street cred by hugging Mike. Reflexively, I punch him. He doesn't move an inch. Make that a centimeter, a millimeter, a nanometer. Whatever tiny fill-in-the-blank-meter measurement you want to use, Mike moves less.

"Okay class, settle down." Dwarfed by Big Mike, Ms. Short speaks as firmly as possible through her happiness. "Michael, it's good to have you here with us. Are you ready to get to work?"

Big Mike nods, drops into the desk directly in

front of me, and the class settles down.

I poke Mike in the back. "What are you doing here?"

"Doctor says I'm clear to go to school," Mike says. "Says my immune system's strong as an ox. Like me."

"Never seen an ox wear a mask."

"Doctor says I've gotta wear it for a while," Mike says. "Just to be careful."

Ms. Short restarts her lesson, attempting to grab the attention of forty-eight eyeballs that all wander in Big Mike's direction.

When the bell rings, everyone surrounds Mike, projectile vomiting questions that Mike tries to answer. They all want more of Big Mike, and he's ready to give it—even if it's just a wink or a wave. Everything he does broadcasts that everything is going to be okay. Big Mike is back, and he's not going anywhere.

In the hallway, it's like a slow-motion movie scene. Every kid freezes, every mouth falls ajar. Mike glides down the hallway, powering through sixth, seventh, and eighth graders who part like the Red Sea.

"That's him!"

"It's Big Mike!"

"That is one big dude!"

"Somebody's not missed many meals."

"It's gotta be him! Look at his hair!"

"He looks so much bigger than he did on stage!"

Big Mike ignores the comments.

"I've been gone almost a year and it was up to you to make sure this place ran well, Carr." He says it making eye contact with his adoring fans. "Looks like you did a decent job. And the girls are still looking fine—though they are a little young for my taste."

I shake my head at Mike's undying love for his blonde nurse.

"Hey, Big Mike!"

Mike looks over his shoulder and stops.

"Cool having you here, man. Real cool."

Mike reaches out his hand to meet Othello's.

"Thanks," Mike says.

"Looks like you shook off cancer pretty easily," Othello says. "Very cool."

Mike shrugs as Vice Principal Confetti bursts through a cluster of eighth grade girls like a hurricane.

"Move it, people!" Mr. Confetti yells. "The tardy bell is about to ring, which means you'll all be late. And I will have no sympathy on any of—

"Michael!" The tone of Mr. Confetti's voice changes from hardened taskmaster to consoling best friend. "You're back! So glad to see you. I heard you had quite a go with everything, but looks like you came out on top. Knew you would!

"And now," he says, waving his hand as if holding Harry Potter's Elder Wand, "get moving!"

The rest of the day repeats this pattern. Everyone—teachers included—can't keep their eyes off Mike. After spending months at home and in the hospital, the only sign that he'd been sick at all was his hair, which is still shaved close. And of course that stylish blue mask.

Lunch is a confusing affair. This year, Mike and I have the same lunch period, which pulls him in two directions: mine and that of his old football team. They stand around a long table, pounding it with their fists and calling his name.

Mike looks at me for direction. I wave him away encouragingly and take my seat with the video game amigos.

Sam points in Mike's direction. "He's back, eh?"

I look over my shoulder at Big Mike, who is surrounded by the football squad. "Looks like it! What's going on over here?"

"Football team wins today," Josh says.

"He can't help that everyone loves him," I say. "Can't get upset because the popular guy doesn't hang out with me all the time."

John's eyes bulge. Leans back as if the walls are falling in on him.

Then, five giant sausage links slam onto my shoulder.

"Want to join us? We've got seats."

Big Mike stands over us, awaiting an answer. Sam, Josh, and John nod their heads in unison. But we're not that desperate.

"Nah," I say. "We're good. Thanks though."

"Oh, come on, Adam." Mike thumbs toward the table of football players. "They want you guys to eat with us."

I eyeball the Sasquatch.

"Seriously," Big Mike says.

I lift my hands in defeat.

thirty-six

"That stuff you did for Mike? Classy stuff, Carr, classy stuff."

Reginald Ellison, the quarterback of the football team, spends the entire lunch telling me how great I am, how he wishes he could have helped Mike out more, that he wishes he lived close enough to hang out with Mike during the rough times, but he takes comfort knowing I was there.

Everyone else—the tight ends, linemen, receivers, corners, and even Mike's replacement nose guard—does the same. It's taken thirteen years, but my brilliance is finally on display at a table of football players, who pour praise on me for my heroic acts. If only they knew my heroism was limited to sitting in Mike's room and reading through his comic books, and that I may be the reason he had to make an emergency trip to the hospital. Oh—and don't forget the time I was so engrossed in my thoughts of Noelle that I didn't realize my best bud was behind me dying. But hey, who am I to rain on their applause parade?

Unfortunately, like all good things, lunch comes to an end. The table of muscle and athleticism breaks camp, the video-game crew and me with them. Lines form in front of teachers.

Over the chatter, teachers sing, "Line up!" to no particular rhythm. Eventually, the students march out of the cafeteria, staying to the right like good middle schoolers.

"Adam Shannon!" pierces through the chaos.

I walk on my tippy toes and crane my neck. Across the cafeteria, Othello stands in line for rectangular pizza, corn, and applesauce.

He waves two fingers and says, "Cool."

On the third day of eating with the football team, a linebacker asks why John, Josh, and Sam never talk. The trio answers with nervous silence.

"Probably don't like talking football and all

143

that," Mike says in their defense. "Am I right?"

Three scrawny deer stand in the headlights of Mike's gaze.

"They like something better, I'd guess," Mike says. "Video games or—video games it is."

"What game you like to play?"

Josh and Sam look at John and then at Donald Hanes, the wide receiver who asks the question.

John says, "Halo, Call of Duty, Skyrim…"

"You don't like any of the older stuff?" Donald asks. "Just those new ones?"

John's eyeballs drift to the ceiling.

"Used to play a lot of Street Fighter," Sam says.

"That the one with Dee Jay? That's a dude I can relate to," Reginald says, rubbing his dark arms with pride.

"You relate to a video-game character? Just because he's black?" Mike says.

"Who said anything about him being black?" Reginald asks. "I relate 'cause dude is ripped!"

With that, it's like I'm back at my old lunch table, listening to people talk about stuff I don't know about. All thanks to my parents' tree-hugging passion.

thirty-seven

I climb the steps of the bus, a.k.a. the big cheese, and wade through a sea of legs outstretched in the middle of the aisle until I reach an empty seat three rows from the back.

I throw my backpack down and turn to see if there is anyone to talk to or if it's going to be a lean-back-and-stay-quiet day.

As I look, a surge of sound washes over the bus. It begins at the front and pushes to the back. Everyone stands and reaches out toward the aisle. I prop myself on one knee to see Big Mike walking toward me—not wearing a mask.

He shakes his bear paw at me and pushes to get

a seat near me.

"What's up?" he asks as the bus door swings closed.

"Hey! Get quiet!" Ms. Delgado's husky yelling voice is accented by a mole dancing below her left nostril. "The year's almost over—I get it! But you still gotta quiet down!"

Once relative quiet reigns, she continues.

"I don't know if y'all noticed, but we got somebody special on this bus. Somebody who ain't been on here for a long, long time. Big Mike," she says, her voice softening, "welcome back. Good to see you, kid."

Mike tips an imaginary hat toward the bus driver. She curtsies.

"So now, in honor of Mike's return, I'd like y'all to close your windows." Nobody moves. "Go on," Ms. Delgado says, "close 'em. Ain't got all day. Gotta get you home before you go gray."

"Put the windows up?"

Ms. Delgado's look ensures this is the only question asked. The bus windows slide up, some with ease, others with a frustrating wiggle and squiggle.

"They all up? Good. Now, take a few sheets of paper out of your backpack. You can grab two, three, twenty—I really don't care. Just grab however much you think you need and wad them up into little balls. There are only three rules to this game. Number one: No throwing paper balls at the bus driver. That's me. Number two: You've gotta clean up a few balls before you get off the bus. Number three: If someone doesn't want to play, you leave 'em alone. Deal?"

Ms. Delgado and her mole drop into the driver's command center, release the emergency brake, and shift the bus into drive.

Before we're out of the bus circle at Palmetto Middle, 4.3 million paper bombs fly through the air. Grenades go off at my side, while rockets whistle through the air and collide against cheeks, foreheads, and throats. Some slap into chests, arms, and guts—solid hits that leave their targets maimed.

Most soldiers sink deep into their bus-seat bunkers, cautiously throwing paper, while shielding themselves from attack. Not Big Mike. He stands fearlessly, sending rockets at a steep decline and an amazing speed, hitting one, two, three, four, five targets in a row. Below him, a sea of arms safeguards faces, while reams of wadded papers float through the air.

His back to me, I drill Big Mike in the back, the shoulder, and finally the back of the head. The last shot gets his attention. He whips around and lets a crumpled-up paper wad rip. His missile screams past me and connects with Misti Miller, who does what Misti Miller always does: she yelps in pain and whimpers.

"Hey! Who's back there crying?" Ms. Delgado eyes the length and breadth of the bus with her gigantic rearview mirror until she sees Misti. "You okay there, sweetie?"

Misti's blonde bangs bounce as she surprisingly nods yes.

"Game on, then!"

At Ms. Delgado's announcement, paper flies even faster. Every few minutes, a ceasefire is called as we approach the home of another injured warrior. One at a time, soldiers dismount the bus, discharged to civilian life.

When Misti's bus stop comes, Big Mike calls her name. Misti winces at an imagined projectile.

"Sorry," he says.

Misti's terror morphs into physical joy. Her body relaxes and then stiffens, as she straightens her body into a rigid example of perfect posture.

"Thank you, Michael," she says with the tone of a substitute teacher. "That is very big of you. I forgive you, and I am glad that you're feeling better."

With that, Misti turns and exits the bus. A few steps away, she turns to wave good-bye to the bus and who she suspects is her newest best friend: the biggest ogre to ever ride Bus 44.

"That is very big of you," I mimic.

But Mike doesn't hear me. He's pressed against the closed bus window, watching Misti disappear. Mike lifts his hand to Misti, who shrinks in the distance, while shells explode around him and rockets scream past his ears. A shot to the head brings Big Mike back to reality, which he enters with a hoot, a holler, and a lightning-fast throw into a sixth grader's chest.

thirty-eight

The last few weeks of school pass like the others. We have classwork. We have homework. And we have an occasional paper fight on the bus.

Whenever Mike's hair struggles to the surface, he shaves it again. At school, he says he does it because the ladies like it, and Misti does seem fond of it. But when it's just us, he admits he doesn't want to let it grow out. At least not until it won't look like a desert wasteland.

The EOC exams that were so eventful last year go by without a hitch. All the bubbles get filled in and the pages and pages and pages of them get passed to the front of classrooms across PMS. Mom takes them up for some teacher, but it isn't mine, so I'm not too concerned about another one of those end-of-the-year embarrassing moments.

End-of-Course exams (EOCs) complete, it's time for end-of-the year locker cleaning. For some, this is the most dreaded part of the school year. They spend months covering their lockers with stickers and taped pictures of pop singers and athletes. Since I only put books in my locker, cleaning it's easy. All I have to do is return my books and give the locker a good wipe down.

I squeeze the 409 trigger when a hand caresses mine. I turn.

It's Noelle.

Noelle Kellogg.

My future bride.

She stares at our hands and asks if she can borrow the 409 for a quick locker cleaning. I oblige.

Maybe this year isn't such a waste after all. And maybe this locker will hold a worthwhile memory, one I'll eventually share with my grandchildren—how their grandmother came and gently held my hand and nearly swooned over me on the last day of school. I'll exaggerate a little, but that's expected with a decent story. What's not expected is the fist that slams into locker 364, right next to my head.

"Aren't you supposed to be cleaning?" Big Mike asks. He follows my line of sight, spins to lean against the locker, and grins. "Ah. Never mind, lover boy. Or should I call you 'dream lover boy'?"

"Call me what?" My cheeks burn, and I wish my hair still covered my entire face.

I slowly return my gaze to Noelle.

"Oh, yeah. Guess she's there, isn't she? Yeah… where's your lady? Oh yeah," I say, "she's probably hanging out at another hospital or something. Looking after some other bald guy. Or maybe you've given up on old ladies and have a thing for Misti now."

Mike puts up his dukes.

"Why, I oughta…"

"Here's the 409, Adam." Noelle holds the bottle out toward me.

"Thanks," I say weakly. "Did it, um, hope it, um, get your locker clean."

Noelle laughs, waves to a friend, moves on. Mike turns to me and acts like his mouth doesn't work.

"Did it, um, I, um, uh, um…"

I go back to cleaning my locker. Mike keeps up the imitations.

thirty-nine

This year wasn't the easiest I've ever had. Sure, it was a breeze academically. But Grandpa—the only roommate I've ever had, the man who helped save my parents' marriage and was loved by everyone he met—died, cancer had to be beaten, I was thrust into the popular group only to realize they were just like the video-game crew, and my relationship with Noelle only took the slightest baby step possible.

So I admit it—maybe I didn't change the world. But I think I may have helped. A little bit at least. And that's gotta count for something.

one

"Settle what?"

"Grandpa's estate." Dad looks exhausted. "Sorry, son. It's legal talk for his stuff—his money, insurance, house. And it's the house that will take us a while to figure out."

"What makes it so hard to figure out his house?" I ask. "We're sitting in it."

Dad exhales heavily.

Mom cuts in.

"Grandpa left the house to us in his will, sweetheart, but we've got to figure out what to do with it."

I save my breath and wrinkle my face in question.

I'M 14 YEARS OLD

Dad answers: "We've got to figure out if we want to stay here or sell it and move."

My heart drops. I feel sick to my stomach.

"Move?"

To be continued...

THANKS

Jessica Brantley and Jonathan Cavett—for making significant changes to the shape of this book. Without you, the story of Adam Shannon Dakota Carr would be as flat as my singing voice.

Jenny Havron—for explaining that I set up a hard-to-escape medical dilemma.

Dr. Larry Swan—for providing an escape route.

My family—for support. My wife (yes, I'm thanking her twice) was particularly helpful with her editing suggestions. Be thankful you didn't see the first draft. It was rough.

Christyne Morrell—for last-minute edits that helped clarify and improve the book, while helping me avoid looking like a jerk.

You—for spending your hard-earned money on this book. I don't take that lightly, and I hope you got your money's worth.

ABOUT THE AUTHOR

D.K. Brantley writes in his dining room, kitchen, bedroom, living room, and basement. He has even spent a fair amount of time writing in the food court of his local mall. He lives in Cleveland, Tennessee, with his wife, their two children, and a miniature Schnauzer.

OTHER BOOKS BY D.K. Brantley

I'm 12 Years Old And I Saved The World

I've got a super lame cell phone and Mom won't let me cut my hair. As if things aren't bad enough, Dad loses his job and Mom and Dad's marriage is on the rocks. Now it's up to me to fix everything. That's right—I'm 12 years old, and I'm about to save the world.

The Only Magic Book You'll Never Need

By D.K. Brantley
Illustrated by Ekaterina Khozatskaya

Not for the faint of heart, weak of knee, incontinent of bladder, or student of Hogwarts, this book teaches you to cauterize a severed torso, turn friends into enemies using super glue and headphones, and more. Becoming an illusionist has never been so impossible, dangerous, or funny.